A Christmas to Dismember

Country Cottage Mystery #12

Addison Moore

and

Bellamy Bloom

Edited by Paige Maroney Smith
Cover by Lou Harper, Cover Affairs
Published by Hollis Thatcher Press, LTD.

Copyright © 2020 by Addison Moore, Bellamy Bloom

This novel is a work of fiction. Any resemblance to peoples either living or deceased is purely coincidental. Names, places, and characters are figments of the author's imagination. The author holds all rights to this work. It is illegal to reproduce this novel without written expressed consent from the author herself.

All Rights Reserved.

Books by the Authors

Cozy Mysteries

Country Cottage Mysteries
Kittyzen's Arrest (Country Cottage Mysteries 1)
Dog Days of Murder (Country Cottage Mysteries 2)
Santa Claws Calamity (Country Cottage Mysteries 3)
Bow Wow Big House (Country Cottage Mysteries 4)
Murder Bites (Country Cottage Mysteries 5)
Felines and Fatalities (Country Cottage Mysteries 6)
A Killer Tail (Country Cottage Mysteries 7)
Cat Scratch Cleaver (Country Cottage Mysteries 8)
Just Buried (Country Cottage Mysteries 9)
Butchered After Bark (Country Cottage Mysteries 10)
A Frightening Fangs-giving (Country Cottage Mysteries 11)
A Christmas to Dismember (Country Cottage Mysteries 12)
Sealed with a Hiss (Country Cottage Mysteries 13)

Meow for Murder
An Awful Cat-titude (Meow for Murder #1)
A Dreadful Meow-ment (Meow for Murder 2)
A Claw-some Affair (Meow for Murder 3)
A Haunted Hallow-whiskers (Meow for Murder 4)

A Candy Cane Cat-astrophe (Meow for Murder 5)

Murder in the Mix

Cutie Pies and Deadly Lies (Murder in the Mix 1)
Bobbing for Bodies (Murder in the Mix 2)
Pumpkin Spice Sacrifice (Murder in the Mix 3)
Gingerbread and Deadly Dread (Murder in the Mix 4)
Seven-Layer Slayer (Murder in the Mix 5)
Red Velvet Vengeance (Murder in the Mix 6)
Bloodbaths and Banana Cake (Murder in the Mix 7)
New York Cheesecake Chaos (Murder in the Mix 8)
Lethal Lemon Bars (Murder in the Mix 9)
Macaron Massacre (Murder in the Mix 10)
Wedding Cake Carnage (Murder in the Mix 11)
Donut Disaster (Murder in the Mix 12)
Toxic Apple Turnovers (Murder in the Mix 13)
Killer Cupcakes (Murder in the Mix 14)
Pumpkin Pie Parting (Murder in the Mix 15)
Yule Log Eulogy (Murder in the Mix 16)
Pancake Panic (Murder in the Mix 17)
Sugar Cookie Slaughter (Murder in the Mix 18)
Devil's Food Cake Doom (Murder in the Mix 19)
Snickerdoodle Secrets (Murder in the Mix 20)
Strawberry Shortcake Sins (Murder in the Mix 21)
Cake Pop Casualties (Murder in the Mix 22)

Flag Cake Felonies (Murder in the Mix 23)
Peach Cobbler Confessions (Murder in the Mix 24)
Poison Apple Crisp (Murder in the Mix 25) Spooky Spice Cake Curse (Murder in the Mix #26)
Pecan Pie Predicament (Murder in the Mix 27)
Eggnog Trifle Trouble (Murder in the Mix 28)

1

"You are a stunner. Have I mentioned that yet?" The man standing before me at the reception counter gives a little wink as he says it. ***What I wouldn't do to have a night alone with this alley cat.***

He waggles his brows my way and any trace of a smile melts from my face.

My name is Bizzy Baker *Wilder*, and I can read minds. Not every mind, not every time, but it happens, and believe me, it's moments like this that I actually regret my supernatural abilities.

"Yes"—I clear my throat—"actually, you have mentioned that." Twenty-six times and counting. A forced smile stretches across my face as I look at Earl Quinn Bennet, the man who owns the Country Cottage Inn.

I've worked right here at the inn as the manager for a half a decade and only met him once before, about a million moons ago.

Quinn is older—sixties, maybe? Early seventies? But he's still a looker, with sharp features, twinkling devilish blue eyes, and gray stubble on both his crown and his cheeks.

This is his first trip stateside in years, but he did let me know he was coming and that he would be throwing the holiday party to end all holiday parties. And that fact alone explains why I have twelve live reindeer roaming around in a makeshift corral at the front of the inn.

It snowed last light, a bona fide Christmas miracle at our end of coastal Maine, which only adds to the seasonal magic. It's early December, and my team and I have worked triple time to festoon the Country Cottage Inn into a virtual wonderland with enough garland and twinkle lights to wrap around the globe twice. And let's not forget the endless supply of red bows and vibrant poinsettias, the gloriously tall Christmas tree in the foyer, the one in the grand room, the dining room, and the three different evergreen stunners sitting in the ballroom, too.

Speaking of the ballroom, I glance in that direction at the sign in the gilded frame, sitting on an equally gilded easel that reads *Welcome to the Christmas Showcase!*

I tried to get Quinn to nail down a refined name for his big event this evening, but he said it didn't need a fancy name. He also mentioned that his friends were pretentious so he didn't have to be. Although knowing what I do about him, which isn't much, Quinn Bennet has plenty of reasons to be as pretentious as he wants to be—several billion reasons to be exact.

But it's not just Quinn's ritzy friends that he's invited. He asked me to extend the invitation to all of Cider Cove as a way to thank our cozy town for their continued support of the inn. The showcase is set to begin in a little under an hour, and the foyer is bustling with socialites from all over Maine. Our cute little seaside town, Cider Cove, doesn't have too many socialites roaming around in it, but just about everyone I know has shown up for the event regardless.

A tall, burly man in a black suit, red dress shirt, and silver tie steps into the inn. He's stalky, chest as broad as a football player's, somewhat scraggly white beard and bushy brows to match as he heads straight for Quinn with a determined look on his face.

I'll be honest, my first thought is to shout for Jordy. Jordy Crosby is my best friend's brother and my ex-husband of one day—think Vegas, cheap whiskey, and an Elvis impersonator. Jordy also happens to be the handyman at the inn, and if need be *bouncer*, but I'm not entirely sure Jordy could take this husky man all on his own.

The burly man gives Quinn a hard slap on the back, and Quinn's blue eyes bulge from the hearty wallop.

Quinn turns and bursts into a fit of laughter. "I thought I had been hit by a freight train." He laughs as he pulls the burly man into one of those half man-hugs. "You don't know your own strength, my friend. And it's a good thing, too. Keep up the momentum where it counts—as in the business you share with me." He looks my way and points to the burly man before him. "Bizzy, this is my partner in crime, Warwick Tully. Warwick, this is my future bride, Bizzy Baker."

A choking sound comes from me, and I quickly force another smile. "Pleasure to meet you, Warwick." I give his hand a quick shake. "I'm actually a happily married woman." I give a quick wink to Quinn as I say it.

A *newly* married woman at that. It will be three months in a few weeks, and I couldn't be happier to be Jasper Wilder's wife. He's the lead homicide detective down in Seaview County where he's just finishing up a day's work, and to be honest, he couldn't get home soon enough. Quinn just landed stateside this afternoon, and Jasper has yet to meet him.

Quinn belts out a laugh. "A married woman?" He leans my way. "I've never let a little nuptial or two stop me before."

Warwick joins in on the raucous laughter before his soft brown eyes meet up with mine. "This guy has been breaking hearts and *rules* for as long as I've known him. I'd watch out if I were you."

That false smile flickers across my face once again.

Oh, I'll be watching—in the event his hands decide to roam.

Quinn leans in. "Don't worry, sweetheart. Tonight I'm throwing the best holiday party Cider Cove has ever seen." He looks to his friend and hitches his head toward the opulent flocked tree standing near the front windows. "I'm guessing you have the latest Sky phone for me?" He gives the phone in his hand a jostle. "Then there are the details regarding Telenational. Tell me you've heeded my words. Don't hurt our reputation, whatever you do." He sighs deeply. "Let's discuss, shall we?"

"We shall." Warwick cinches a smile of his own. ***Discuss how rotten and evil you can be.*** He laughs to himself as he looks to his old friend and the two of them step away.

My sweet cat, Fish, stretches her front paws across the creamy marble reception counter and lets out a rather ornery meow.

I've about had enough of all this holiday hubbub. Is it Christmas yet?

Fish is a black and white long-haired tabby I found over a couple of years ago near my sister's soap and candle shop, Lather and Light. Fish and I have been as close as sisters ourselves ever since.

I pick her up and land a soft kiss to the top of her head.

"We've got a ways to go yet. But it will be here sooner than you know." Although something tells me not soon enough. It's the busiest time of year for the inn. Just about every room is booked solid with out-of-towners visiting family, and all of the cottages on the property are booked solid, too.

The inn is set on several acres, and there are over three dozen cottages in addition to the mammoth inn itself. The entire structure butts up to a sandy cove where the magnificent Atlantic takes center stage as the star of the show. There's a café attached to the back of the inn that faces the water which I've wisely left my best friend, Emmie, in charge of. And on the opposite end of the facility, we have a pet daycare center that provides daily interaction for the furry inclined among us who would otherwise be left home alone all day while their human goes off to work, or in the event one of the guests needs a pet sitter for the day.

The inn is a mammoth structure composed of blue stones and blue shutters with ivy that covers almost every speck of the front. There's a small army of employees that work alongside me, and each one loves the inn just as much as I do. The Country Cottage Inn was voted the most pet friendly place to stay in all of Maine for a fifth year in a row. I'm actually the one who instated the rule that all pets are welcome on the grounds and in the guests' rooms. Personally, I was shocked it wasn't instated before.

Sherlock scampers over and gives a sharp bark my way. Sherlock Bones was Jasper's red and white mixed puppy when we first met, and now he equally belongs to me. He's medium-size with big brown eyes and a heart for both people and bacon.

I want Christmas to last forever, Bizzy. Everyone is so friendly and I like the music, too.

Fish yowls, **You would.**

I do! Sherlock is quick to double down on his love of all things Christmas. **It's cheerful and snappy, and it makes me want to bounce my bottom and wag my tail.**

I can't help but laugh.

I'm not sure how the animals understand one another, but they always seem to. Yes, I can read the animal mind as well, and typically they have better things to say. I can't read every mind. Usually it's just the ones in front of me, but when I get stressed and frazzled, I'll pick up on a variety of people at once. And the farther away someone is, the harder for me to decipher if it's a man or woman prattling on. It all sounds a little androgynous at that point.

"Bizzy!"

I turn to find my sister, Macy, heading this way. We're both in our late twenties, but she's older than me by a year and sassier than me by a million miles. She dyes her black hair blonde and wears it in a short bob. She looks dressed to kill tonight in a skintight red pantsuit that looks as if she'll have to peel herself out of.

"I want you to meet a friend." Macy pulls a tall brunette with a cranberry smile this way. The woman is wearing the most gorgeous brocade gown I've ever seen. It's black and purple and has just a hint of navy in it. She wears the same hairstyle as Macy—short, blunt bob—her eyes are perfectly almond-shaped, and she has gorgeous olive skin that I would die for. "Bizzy, this is Eve French. She owns that hot new boutique out in Rose Glen, Elora's Closet."

"Nice to meet you," I say.

"Nice to meet *you*, Bizzy." Eve holds out her hand and I shake it. "I met your sister a couple months back at the Businesswomen of Maine Expo, and we've been fast friends ever since." Her eyes flit toward the tree, and her entire body seizes. ***There he is, the rat that ruined me. My goodness, if he isn't as handsome as ever. Oh my heart, how I love him. Oh my heart, how I can't wait to see him suffer.***

Her chest vibrates as she huffs, and I follow her gaze to see her staring intently in the area where Quinn stands.

Another man has joined Quinn and Warwick, a tall, younger man, mid-thirties to early forties. His dark hair is shaved in the back and a little longer in the front, and he has matching dark stubble on his cheeks. The three of them seem to be laughing and having a good time. I wonder which one Eve was talking about?

"Do you know Quinn?" I ask without hesitating. This is his event, after all.

Eve gives a few blinks as if coming to. "You could say I know him." ***Intimately for that matter. Frankly, I'm shocked he had the nerve to show his face after what he did to me.***

So it's Quinn she's pining for—and equally loathing. I can see how that could be a pattern in Quinn's life. He's as adorable as he is deplorable.

Eve nods my way. "It was nice meeting you, Bizzy. I'd better get inside that ballroom. I've got a teenager roaming around in there with her friends." She rolls her eyes to Macy. "Be glad you're not saddled with kids who aren't afraid to talk back."

Macy nods. "Oh, I thank my childless stars every day." She links arms with Eve as they start for the ballroom. "Here's hoping we find some wealthy hot men. That's not too much to ask for this time of year, is it?"

Eve cackles at the thought as they disappear.

Georgie Conner, an eighty-something-year-old hippie that I regard as family, runs into the foyer wearing one of her signature wonky quilt dresses. Ever since Georgie's quilting mishap has taken off, she and my mother have been peddling them like crazy. In fact, they've recently rented a space on Main Street right across from my sister's shop in hopes to hock their wares.

"Bizzy Baker Wilder." Georgie stalks my way with her wild gray hair—think Einstein, but longer—and her lavender-blue eyes narrowed to slits. "Your mother is going to be the death of me," she bleats my way as she takes Fish from me. "The cat is mine for the rest of the night. I'll need her as my emotional support kitty." She drops a kiss to Fish's furry forehead, and Fish mewls back with approval. "You too, fuzz face." She plucks a few pieces of bacon from her pocket and drops them to the floor for Sherlock.

"Georgie, your wonky quilt dress is gorgeous," I muse as I take in the red and green wonder. It's pieced together in large triangular sections with frayed edges and all sorts of fabrics. I can see everything from snowmen to reindeer in them. "But aren't you burning up in that?"

Georgie's wardrobe staple has pretty much been flowing kaftans ever since I've known her. And I've known her since I was a kid. Her daughter Juni, aka Juniper Moonbeam, was married to my father for a short spate of time.

My father collects ex-wives the way some men collect sports cars or hunting trophies. And Juni was simply one in a long line of many women who came after my mother.

Speaking of which, my mother trots up behind Georgie. Mom is petite, still feathers her hair circa 1980-something, and has on a forest green dress embellished with lots of gold jewelry. She's not typically so flashy, but seeing this is turning out to be the flashiest event of the season, it's well warranted.

Mom makes a face at Georgie. "There you are. If I didn't know better, I'd think you were trying to lose me."

Georgie snarls my way. "It didn't work, did it? And you're right, Bizzy. I am burning up in this wonky quilt dress. Because I've got a fire-breathing dragon after me."

Mom's mouth falls open. "Who are you calling a dragon? We just went into business together, and might I remind you, I fronted the capital to do so."

"Oh, you've reminded me, all right, Toots. You remind me in the morning. You remind me in the afternoon. You remind me before I go to bed at night so I can have nightmares of you reminding me." She hitches her thumb my way. "Have you heard? News on the preppy street is your mother wants to name the shop Wonky Quilts and Things. It's *boring*, Bizzy! If I wanted to die a yuppie death, I would have worked as an accountant and paid my taxes a long time ago."

Mom balks at her old friend, "And get a load of this." Mom takes a page out of Georgie's ornery book and hitches her thumb my way. "She wants to name the shop the Dreamcatcher's Hookah Lounge."

"What's wrong with that?" Georgie howls.

"We don't sell hookahs!"

The two of them take off for the ballroom with a start, and I'm not too sorry to see them go.

I spot my best friend, Emmie Crosby, headed this way along with her boyfriend, Leo Granger, and I breathe a sigh of relief. Emmie and I not only share the same black hair and icy blue eyes, but we share the same first name as well, Elizabeth. But to keep things simple, we've gone through life with the nicknames our families gave us and we've never been happier.

Leo, her official plus one, happens to hold my special supernatural ability—that little detail about reading minds. That's how we met about a year ago. Since then, he's fallen in love with my beautiful bestie, and he just let me know about a week ago that he's about to pop the question on Christmas

Eve. Leo has enlisted my help in both finding the perfect ring and helping him pull off the perfect proposal, whatever that might be.

"Bizzy!" Emmie gives me a warm embrace while holding out the platter in her hand brimming with peppermint bark. "Please take one—or take a fistful. You look as if you could use it."

"Can I ever." I quickly snap one up and take a bite of the creamy white and dark chocolate combination, sprinkled with just the right amount of candy cane bits. "*Mmm*, this is to die for."

Leo winces. "Watch what you say." Leo has dark hair and dark eyes, and a dark sense of humor to match. He's a deputy down at the sheriff's department where Jasper works, and I couldn't have picked a better man for Emmie. "I'd like to go at least a month without a homicide."

"You and me both," I tell him as I indulge in another sweet bite of the magic that Emmie has produced en mass for tonight's event. Emmie isn't just in charge of the Country Cottage Café, she pretty much does all the baking. Good thing, because I can't go within ten feet of a stove without burning something in my wake. It's safe to say Emmie shines where I go dim.

Emmie just found out about my mind reading abilities a couple months back, and I'm thankful she's still speaking to me. Only a handful of people know, like Jasper and Georgie, too, and I don't plan on broadening that number anytime soon.

What do you think of this dress? She wiggles her shoulders my way. Emmie has donned a sparkling silver number, with a little more *va-va-voom* than I'm used to seeing on her. I just threw on a simple black dress and called it a night, but I can tell Emmie is set to impress. **Leo's mother will be here tonight, and I want to make a good impression**.

"Oh shoot." She stomps a matching silver heel as she turns to Leo. "I keep forgetting you can hear my thoughts, too. So not fair." She wrinkles her nose at him before going in for a kiss.

"You look stunning," I tell her as my eyes dip to her plunging cleavage. "Maybe ask my mother if she has a brooch in her purse?" I give a little shrug. "If not, I can loan you a paperclip."

"You keep your paperclips to yourself." She gives me a playful swat on the arm. "I'd better get this to the ballroom," she says, holding up the platter in her hands. "I still have three trips to make at least." She takes off and Leo steps in my way.

"You ready for tomorrow?" he asks with a twinge of something that looks to be nerves skirting his face.

"Preston Jewelers, eleven-thirty," I say. "How can I forget?" Actually, I can't forget because I'm also meeting my brother, Huxley, there at the very same time. He, too, is about to ask his girlfriend for her claw, or *hand* as it were, in marriage this Christmas Eve, and he's enlisted me as his consultant as he walks the green mile.

Leo's chest bucks with a laugh. "You really don't care for Mackenzie Woods, do you?"

I'm about to let him know exactly how right he is when Mack and Huxley step this way.

Mackenzie Woods and I grew up together, and we were close up until we weren't. She's a stunning chestnut brunette who happens to be following in the footsteps of her father and her grandfather before that as the acting mayor of Cider Cove.

Huxley Baker is my warm, funny, serial womanizer turned family attorney of a brother. He's handsome with his dark hair and dark smile and has a penchant for making poor decisions, but I won't hold it against him.

Mackenzie bleeds a wicked smile my way. "I heard that comment. Of course she doesn't care for me, Leo. I'm sure she let a real zinger fly. Funny how I don't have any negative things to say behind your back, Bizzy. I save them all to share right in front of your face." She heads my way and leans her lips to my ear. "Any luck getting the class ring?" she whispers through the side of her mouth.

I make a face over at my brother before whispering back, "My mother has it."

Mackenzie nods as she stalks toward the ballroom in a red glitzy dress that garners the attention of every male in the vicinity.

About a week ago Mackenzie clued me in on the fact *she* plans on proposing to my brother come Christmas Eve. Little does she know he plans on proposing to her on the very same night. I'm not sure why, but a part of me feels as if things will go explosively wrong. Most things do when Mackenzie is involved.

Hux growls, "Good going, Biz. Whatever you whispered to her really ticked her off. Keep up the good work and she'll want to divorce me before I get to pop the question." He takes off after her.

"That's not what happened," I shout after him.

Leo chuckles. "I have a feeling his entire future will involve chasing her and wondering what ticked her off. See you inside." He takes off, and I'm about to follow him when I spot a blonde with dark-framed glasses glaring at the trio of men by the tree with a look that could slice a mountain down the middle. She's wearing a heavy red gown that looks as if it's comprised solely of red rubies, and it glitters with her every move.

I step her way and smile. "Can I help you?"

Her affect brightens once I manage to steal her attention.

"Yes, actually. I'm Angelica Chatfield." Her lips crimp. "I'm a part of the production tonight and wanted to see where I should go to prepare." Her eyes stray back to Quinn and his guests as they share a riotous laugh. ***Prepare to kill perhaps. Or should I say, prepare to die? I'll have your head on a platter tonight, my friend.***

My lips part as a breath hitches in my throat at the ornery thought.

"Right this way," I say, leading her away from those men, one of which has really lit her fuse. "The ballroom is waiting for you."

Tonight promises to bring merriment and pleasure.

Let's just hope it doesn't bring murder, too.

2

The ballroom at the Country Cottage Inn sparkles with holiday magic from both the crystal chandeliers to the *three* fifteen-foot tall evergreens festooned with every Christmas bauble and twinkle light this season calls for.

Quinn emailed me a list of instructions long before he ever touched down this afternoon regarding every last detail of today's event, from the live reindeer out front to the stage he had Jordy construct in the front of the room, complete with black velvet curtains to close between acts. I'm going to keep the setup because it's just so gorgeous, and I'm sure I can utilize it for many events to come.

Quinn hired a theater company to arrange all of the acts and deliver props and stage decorations, and they've been in and out all week working hard to make the magic happen. The backdrop set across the stage is a well-lit flocked Christmas tree with large boxes set around it, each wrapped in red and green foil. There's even a crew here just for the lighting, and it looks as if we're about to be treated to a genuine holiday extravaganza. It reminds me of when I was young, my mother would take us to see *The Nutcracker* every year. How I miss that, and now thanks to Quinn, I have some of that holiday magic back again.

"Here Comes Santa Claus" plays softly over the speakers as throngs of exquisitely dressed people mingle freely. I've never seen so many designer holiday dresses and men in suits with gleaming silk ties. The refreshment table is laden with Christmas cookies from the Country Cottage Café and, of course, the platters of Emmie's peppermint bark are quickly being depleted. I'm sort of a disaster in the kitchen, contrary to my maiden name, but that's what best friends are for, and quite literally in this situation, seeing that she's the head baker and manager of the café. Rows and rows of chairs have been set out, some of which are already filled, and a thicket of people are milling around on the stage as well.

I spot Georgie and Juni near the front with a small crowd of women gathered around them. Most of the women are lavishing attention on Fish and Sherlock, both of which appear to be in back scratch heaven. And by the looks of it, Georgie has convinced Juni to put on one of her wonky quilt dresses as well. Juni pretty much is a duplicate of Georgie, but her hair is light brown with far less gray, and her face has a few less wrinkles. That quilt dress she's donned isn't Juni's usual fare.

She's more of a leather and lace girl, but it's nice to see her teaming up with her mama to peddle her wares.

But something to the right of them catches my eye, and I crane my neck to get a better look. Standing just behind the heavily flocked evergreen with its bright red ornaments, I see Quinn and that blonde woman with the dark-framed glasses, Angelica, having what looks to be a tense conversation. He sets his coffee down on the small table behind them laden with hot cocoa and a plate of sweet treats. They're props for one of the acts, but I happen to know they're real because Emmie and I placed them there earlier. Angelica picks up a cookie and takes a bite just as a one of the stagehands comes over and steals Quinn away for a moment. Angelica watches them go before quickly rummaging for something in her purse, and then her hand moves over Quinn's coffee as if she were shaking something into it.

Every muscle in my body freezes.

Did she just spike his drink?

Quinn reappears and picks up his drink, taking a sip without missing a beat.

"Bizzy!" Macy strides up with her friend Eve in tow, and this time there's a teenage girl with them who shares Eve's glossy dark hair and almond-shaped eyes. All three of them have a small dessert plate filled with goodies but mostly with Emmie's peppermint bark. "I *must* sell this in my shop." Macy holds up a shard of peppermint bark my way.

Eve nods. "I want in on this deliciousness, too. My customers would buy boxes of this by the dozen. And this is the best I've ever tasted." Her eyes drift over my shoulder and she gives a light gasp. ***And finally we meet again. Now to let him have it.*** "Would you ladies excuse me a moment?" She darts off, and I turn to see her heading straight for my dapper boss.

Macy shrugs. "Bizzy, this is Elsie, Eve's daughter." She turns to the girl. "How old are you again?"

"Fifteen." She rolls her eyes at Macy, and I can't help but chuckle at her teen-sponsored enthusiasm.

"Nice to meet you, Elsie. I'm Bizzy. I run the inn. Quinn, the man that's putting on the event tonight, is my boss. So I take it your mom knows Quinn?" I know so much because she told me so herself when we met in the lobby. "Did she work for him at one time?"

"I don't know anything about her working for him." She tugs on a lock of her hair as she glances their way. "But she's, like, low-key thirsting on him. It's been going on for years. She's convinced he should have been my daddy." She says *daddy* in air quotes. "But he's not, and I think she blames him for everything that's gone wrong for her. But don't worry. My mom is a pro at revenge." She gives a wild wave to someone behind me and takes off screaming with laughter.

Macy makes a face. "I need that kind of energy."

"What did she mean by 'low-key thirsting on him'?"

"Who knows?" Macy shudders. "This is why I don't have kids. I don't have the energy to decode what they're trying to say. Which brings me to my next point—have a couple of kids already, would you? I can't be the cool aunt without a crew of littles to be cool to. By the way, they're missing out on some majorly awesome gifts this year. I had an opportunity to snatch up one of those hard to find game consoles." Her attention quickly gets hijacked to something or someone behind me. "Ooh, I see a *hottie*, and I bet he rides a Ducati. This place is crawling with billionaires. Good work on hauling in the upper echelon. How much do you charge for this dating service? Never mind. I'm family. Wish me luck." She darts off, and I follow her with my gaze, only to see her stop cold in front of that man with the partially shorn head of hair that was speaking to Quinn out in the lobby.

I can't help but shake my head at my lust-driven sister. I have to give her credit, she doesn't miss a beat when a good-looking man is in the vicinity. Here's hoping he's unattached. I'm not sure what my sister's boundaries are anymore. My eyes drift toward the crowd, and I spot a tall, dark, and unstoppably handsome homicide detective headed this way.

Jasper's lids hood over his lightning gray eyes, his dark hair is freshly slicked back, and he slays in a dark suit with a crimson tie. And as he strides past the masses, an entire line of socialites is left fanning themselves in his wake.

His lips curl up with wicked intent. "Kiss me if I'm wrong, but those reindeer out front really do know how to fly."

"Ha-ha, very funny," I say, pulling him in by the tie. "You should be careful when hitting on women like that. There's a hot homicide detective who happens to find his way into my bed every night—lucky, *lucky* me. He's liable to arrest you. And have I mentioned he shoots on sight?"

He pretends to frown. "Maybe I should call the cops and have you arrested?" He glances down at my dress that hugs my curves in all the right places. "Because it's illegal to look this good." Jasper comes in for a kiss, and I don't stop him. Instead, I reward him with something to look forward to.

"Macy thinks we should start on a couple of kids." I bite down a smile. "But I'm not quite ready for them."

He feigns disappointment. "I'm not either, but you know what they say, practice makes perfect. No point in not trying." He waggles his brows. "I'll boot that homicide detective from your bed tonight and we'll get cracking at it."

A laugh pumps from me, and I turn my head slightly and spot Quinn by the refreshment table with that man Macy was trying to hit on. The man looks red-faced and angry, and Quinn looks disturbed as well.

"I don't think Quinn is having the best night," I say to Jasper, and he turns their way.

Warwick, the stalky man with the white beard I met earlier, steps between the arguing men and the younger man leaves in a huff. Warwick jabs a finger in Quinn's chest as they exchange a few words of their own, and soon Warwick takes off in the opposite direction.

Quinn's eyes drift my way and he manufactures a smile for both Jasper and me, raising his cup our way before taking a sip.

"Oh, I'm so embarrassed," I say to Jasper as a crowd moves between my poor boss and us. "That man traveled all this way. I hope he has a good time tonight."

Jasper's chest widens as he scans the room. "How can he not? He's surrounded by five hundred of his closest friends and you, his beautiful manager."

"Therein lies the problem. Have I mentioned that he hasn't stopped hitting on me since he arrived?"

Jasper's eyes widen. "The man dies tonight."

The lights flicker, and everyone scurries to their seats, including Jasper and me. The curtains close for a moment then reopen with a single spotlight shining down on the stage as the rest of the room remains enveloped with darkness. Soon, we're treated to an adorable play about Santa getting stuck in the chimney and watch as a group of teenagers uses an axe to break him free.

An elegant choir is up next, each member in a pristine cranberry colored robe as they sing an awe-inspiring rendition of "Silent Night".

A few more skits take place, and there's even a comedian who takes the stage, leaving us all in stitches. But the pièce de résistance is the lady in the dress that looked as if it was comprised of red rubies, the woman I met in the lobby, the one who looked as if she was slipping a mickey into Quinn's coffee,

Angelica Chatfield.

She sings a stunning aria that brings everyone to their feet once she's through. The last to rise from his seat is the guest of honor himself, Quinn Bennet. His arms remain folded across his chest as the rest of the room breaks out into a raucous applause.

His behavior seems odd. Disturbing even. Hers was the best performance of the night by far.

The applause dies down, and Quinn heads to the stage, bowing slightly to Angelica as she speeds to the audience with her chin in the air. It's clear she didn't take too well to his snubbing.

"Thank you all for coming out tonight," he says above a whisper into the microphone. The dramatic lighting only magnifies his dashing good looks. "How about another round of applause for the effervescent Angelica Chatfield?" Another short-lived round of applause circles the room. "Angelica always did know how to bring the men to their feet." A burst of laughter erupts from the crowd, and I glance to Angelica seated in front and she doesn't look amused in the slightest.

Quinn lowers his hand to the crowd, and everyone finds their seats once again.

"I want to give a special thank you to Bizzy Baker and the wonderful staff at the Country Cottage Inn. Out of all of my holdings, this treasure on the Atlantic has always held a special place in my heart." Another light round of applause breaks out.

I give Jasper's hand a squeeze as I lean in and whisper, "I swear I told him my last name was Wilder twenty times."

It's easier to hit on a married woman if you deny her husband exists.

I nod up at him because I think he's onto something.

Quinn needles his gaze to his left. "And if Arthur Silver would please stand. If anyone deserves a trophy for dealing with me, it's this man. Arthur is my accounts manager. He makes sure the bills are paid, and more importantly, he slips all of the beautiful women my phone number."

A round of laughter ensues as the man Macy was hitting on pops out of his seat for a moment.

Quinn chortles as he glances out at the crowd. "Of course, we wouldn't end the night without a proper thank you to Warwick, whom many of you know as the sharpest knife in just about any room. Don't turn your back or he might just cut you with it. Warwick, my old friend, I couldn't be happier to see your smiling face tonight. You never fail to do what's right. And you won't."

"That's right." Warwick waves to the crowd from the second row. "I keep the numbers of the beautiful women to myself."

The crowd breaks out into a fit of laughter once again, and Jasper and I join in on it. Warwick seems like a decent guy. I'm glad Quinn has good friends in the States.

"Yes, well"—Quinn looks dead ahead at someone seated in the front row, and I follow his gaze to Eve French—"some beautiful women refuse to stop throwing themselves my way." He gives a little wink, but a bite of embarrassment spears through me for the poor woman.

The sound of a bell ringing comes from the right and in walks Santa Claus, dressed in his traditional red suit. He has a snow-white beard and a velvet sack is attached to his back.

"Ho ho ho!" Santa belts it out like the pro he is. "Have we all been good girls and boys?"

The crowd responds with a resounding *yes*.

"Well, I have a few treats for you." Santa opens his sack, and before we know it, it's raining candy canes and small stuffed animals as the crowd goes wild to catch them. "And Quinn, it's nice to see you've landed on this side of the pond. You've saved me a trip." He lifts a finger. "Never mind. You were on the naughty list this year."

The audience thunders with laughter.

"Ah, wait a minute, wait a minute." Santa waves a hand to the crowd and the volume dies down. "I was thinking of another Quinn Bennet. You were actually an exemplary individual this year." He gives a hard wink our way, much to the delight of the crowd. "You've given a lot to a lot of people, Quinn. And for that reason, I have a very special gift for you." He pulls a large red and white checkered box out of his sack and sets it on the floor.

Quinn twitches his lips at the sight. "Let me guess. The world's smallest woman?"

A few snickers circle the room, and I make a face at

Jasper.

Who knew Quinn Bennet was such a woman-hungry beast?

Quinn lifts the lid off the box and out pops the head of the world's cutest blond puppy complete with a red ball on his nose that's blinking on and off. There's a red satin bow tied around his neck and he looks like the quintessential Christmas puppy.

The crowd loses it in a mixture of laughter and coos as Quinn picks the puppy up and cradles it in his arms.

Quinn looks to the crowd. "Now that Rudolph has arrived, I think we can really start this party. Enjoy your evening, everyone. Please, stop by and say hello to Rudolph and Santa before you leave." The house lights come back on, and soon the room is swirling with conversations and errant laughter.

Cheery Christmas carols bleat through the speakers and people are mobbing the refreshment tables once again.

The night wears on and the crowd doesn't thin one bit. Jasper and I make the rounds and talk to Leo and Emmie, Hux and Mackenzie, and we even spot my father and Jasper's mother from across the room.

Just as we're about to head that way, Sherlock and Fish run over. Sherlock is dancing a little jig as I scoop Fish up in my arms.

She mewls as she rubs her head over my chest. ***He's going to have an accident if you don't do something*** *quickly. Do they make diapers for dogs? Because at this rate he'll need them.*

Sherlock gives a soft bark. ***Someone spilled some water and I was kind enough to help get it off the floor. I can't help it. That stuff goes right through me.***

Jasper twists his lips down at his cute pooch. "I don't need to be a mind reader to know what he needs. I'll take him out to the garden."

"I'll go with you."

We exit through the side door that leads to a dark wooded area with a fountain illuminating the blue cobbled path that snakes throughout the property. The moon is high overhead, it's bitter cold and snowy out, and the only sound is the quiet rush of that fountain.

"It's bliss out here," I say as Fish jumps out of my arms.

Sherlock trots off to the grass to our left just as Fish lets out a sharp yowl.

Bizzy, I think you need to see this. She jumps on all fours with her back arched, her fur standing on end.

"Hey"—I quickly make my way over to the fountain where she stands frozen solid on the edge of the bottom tier—"what's the matter? Is the water splashing you a bit too much?" I'm about to pick her up when I spot what looks to be a hand floating in the fountain as the water swirls pink around it. "Jasper?" I call him over. "Do you think this is left over from

Halloween?" I'm not sure why I asked the question, but my mind demands I make sense of the sight.

"Let's find out." He picks a stick off the ground and is about to jab at it when Sherlock lets out several riotous barks at something near the woods and I spot that sweet puppy with its red ribbon tied around his collar and that red plastic nose of his blinking on and off like a beacon.

Jasper and I head that way and I gasp at the sight.

Lying on the ground is Quinn Bennet with his eyes open as he looks to the sky, the blade of an axe buried deep in his chest, and his left hand is noticeably and horrifically missing.

Quinn Bennet isn't going to have to worry about throwing the best holiday party Cider Cove has ever seen.

Quinn Bennet is dead.

3

"He's dead," I pant the words out as Jasper pulls me a few feet away.

"I'm sorry, Bizzy," Jasper says as he looks past me over at the body. "I'm going to call it in. I need you to take the animals out of here. I'll text Leo. Stay safe and stay away from anyone acting suspiciously."

Jasper takes a few steps back toward the corpse as he quickly makes that call, and I take the moment to sweep the area with my gaze.

Dotting the lapel of Quinn's suit jacket is a single red bead, the color of blood, and in the shape of a tear. I have a feeling I know exactly where that came from—Angelica Chatfield's dress. A single white glove lies a few feet away, smeared with blood on it. And just behind that there are tiny paw prints in the snow that lead right up to the special angel Santa gifted to Quinn earlier this evening.

"Come here, sweetie," I say, carefully making a circle around Quinn as I scoop the shivering sweet baby boy off the snow. I gather Fish in my other arm and Sherlock bounds up next to me. "Jasper, there's a red bead on his jacket." The words stream frantically from me. "And there's a glove next to the body. And his hand, it's—"

"I know." He looks up from the phone and nods just as the area is miraculously flooded with deputies.

My feet carry me inside to the bustle of voices, now sounding far more worried than they are merry, just as Leo finishes speaking to the crowd from the stage.

The puppy barks then whimpers and Fish pats him gently on the nose.

My name is Fish, and the moving carpet is Sherlock Bones. And don't worry about the woman carrying you. Her name is Bizzy and she can hear your thoughts and mine.

Sherlock barks up at us. ***She can understand you, too.***

Fish lets out a gurgle of a meow. ***Only if you're saying something intelligible.***

The tiny pup growls and whimpers. ***I don't know what to think. I don't know what to do or say. Where is that ball they put on my nose? I just want to chew on it and go back to sleep.***

"Rudolph?" I look into his sweet brown eyes. "Do you mind if I call you that?"

He gives a soft bark. *I don't see why not. I have no other name.*

"I'm sorry you had to witness that," I whisper. "Did you happen to see anyone out there with Quinn before he—"

Fell? He barks.

I nod. We'll go with that.

The cute puppy squirms as he glances to the ceiling. *I heard voices. A man and a woman.*

"A woman was talking to Quinn?"

A woman was talking to another man. I didn't see their faces, and then I got lost in the woods. When I came back, Quinn was already asleep.

Sherlock moans. *A woman and a man. There could have been two killers.*

Fish pats Rudolph on the head with her tail. *It doesn't matter if there were twenty killers, Rudolph. Bizzy could find them all.*

"Here's hoping I can track down whoever did this no matter how many guilty parties there are. He was the owner of this inn. My boss. This just got personal."

The murmurs in the room grow to impossible decibels as Georgie swoops over with Juni in tow.

"Give me a baby." Georgie plucks Rudolph right out of my hands. "Something has gone terribly wrong, Bizzy. There's a bomb on the premises."

"A *what*?" I squawk in disbelief.

"No, no." Juni bats her away. "Some teenager said *this* was the bomb. There's a body on the grounds. Leo says there's been a crime committed. Rumors are circulating that there's a jewel thief in the room. Trust me, there's no better way to get a bunch of rich people hopped up in fear than threatening to strip them of their diamonds." She chuckles at the thought. **I've done it a few times myself.**

Figures.

Georgie holds Rudolph against her shoulder and pats his back as if trying to comfort him just as my mother strides up.

"Are you trying to burp him or beat him?" Mom excavates Rudolph from Georgie's arms. "Come here, you poor sweet thing. Bizzy, where is Quinn Bennet? I'd like to give him an official invite to our store opening next week. I bet an entire honey hive of socialites will follow him over. Not to mention it'll be the bees knees to be seen at our place after that." She swats Juni and they share a cackle.

Juni shakes her head. "That man ain't showin' up to no quilt shop. I've met men like Quinn before. He won't even look in that direction unless you've got a young hot thing standing naked in your storefront."

"Good idea." Mom snaps her fingers. "Bizzy, what are you doing a week from today?"

"Funny, Mother," I say, and Fish chortles as if she thought it was hilarious, too.

Fish presses her paws against my chest. **You'd have no problem walking around in the nude if you just stop**

shaving. Take a break from the razor and I bet you'll sprout fur all over in no time.

"That's what I'm afraid of," I whisper.

"What's that?" Mom tips her ear my way. "What's going on here, Bizzy? I have my cats to get home to and Leo just announced we're not allowed to leave the building. I think we all know I'd make a jewel thief pretty unhappy." She holds up her bare left hand. "So if you don't mind, I'd like to cut out early."

"It has nothing to do with jewelry," I say. "Something happened to Quinn."

Juni sucks in a quick breath. "They've kidnapped him!"

"Kidnapped who?" someone in the crowd shouts.

"Nobody," I shout back, half-afraid I'll set the room ablaze with rumors. "The sheriff's department has it all handled."

Georgie grunts, "Haven't you learned anything by now, Bizzy? You need to give the people answers before things get wildly out of control. She cups her hand to her mouth. "They've captured your leader and they're coming for the rest of you!"

A round of gasps goes off in the room, followed by dramatic murmuring.

Juni cups her mouth as well and I cringe. "And they've unleashed an army of mice in the room, too!"

Half the women hop onto a chair and scream, and I'm half-tempted to join them.

"Would you hush!" I shoot the mother-daughter rumormongering duo a look before I step deeper into the room. "Um, hello," I shout and garner everyone's attention at once. "I'm Bizzy Baker—um, Wilder..." Good Lord, I don't know if I can ever get used to having three names. It's certainly not convenient when shouting at a panicked crowd. "I'm sorry to inform you, but a very serious crime has been committed on the premises."

A woman with a gold dress lets out a harrowing cry. "We're being held hostage, aren't we?"

"What?" I glance to Leo who is quickly making his way in this direction while slitting his throat with his finger in an effort to stop me from making it worse. "No. There are no terrorists." Or at least I hope not.

"Then there's a burglary in process," someone else shouts.

"No," I'm quick to answer. "Not that. I promise. You're all safe."

Fish purrs, *As safe as they can be with a killer on the loose.*

Sherlock whimpers, *A killer who wants to chop us all to pieces.*

"Is there a killer on the loose?" someone shouts from afar, and I open my mouth then close it.

"There is! Isn't there?" the woman in the gold dress howls, and I cringe because I can't bring myself to lie to these people.

Macy and Eve French step this way.

"*Bizzy?*" Macy hisses with that annoyed look she gets when I'm embarrassing her. "Say something or these people are going to think there's a killer on the loose."

Eve gasps. "You can't deny it, can you?" Her eyes round out. "There's been a murder!"

The word *murder* echoes around the room like a demonic whisper.

Warwick staggers forward as if he were mortally wounded himself. "Who's been killed?" he shouts as if speaking for the rest of crowd, and at this point he pretty much is.

The blonde woman, Angelica, the one who sang that gorgeous rendition of "Silent Night," traipses forward.

"Where's Quinn?" She gives a frenetic glance around. "My goodness, it was Quinn, wasn't it?"

Leo tweaks his brows at me. **Way to keep the crowd under control.**

I shoot him a look. **Ironically, that was your job.**

Eve staggers forward. "Is it true? Is Quinn Bennet dead?" Her eyes are wide, her chest heaving with her every breath.

"It's true," I hear myself say, regardless if I wanted to or not. It seemed inevitable, inescapable even.

Warwick clutches at his chest. "My dear friend." **You've met your fate at last.**

Eve nods as if she heard his inner rambling. **A loss or a gain for the world... I can't quite decide.**

Angelica's lips flicker. ***And now to relax until the reading of the will. It's shaping up to be the best holiday season yet.***

The room stirs with conversation as the words *dead, Quinn Bennet,* and *reading of the will* go off like the chorus to a very sad song—with the exception that no one seems particularly sad about it.

A swarm of deputies enters the room, and soon they're taking the names and numbers of those in attendance.

Who knew my wildest dream would come true tonight? a voice calls out from deep in the heart of this madness, and I can't tell if it was a woman or a man.

How I hope he left it all to me. I deserve it—hell, I've earned it, another voice adds to the chaos.

A woman lets out a whoop of a cry just a few feet away, and I look over to find Georgie with that wonky quilt dress that was once on her now clutched in her hand while she waves it over her body like the flag of surrender.

"Oh dear Lord, no." I groan. Georgie has stripped herself bare, with the exception of what looks to be a dingy white bathing suit of some sort—a one-piece thankfully.

Leo groans at the sight as well. ***What do you think, Bizzy? Should I arrest her for public nudity?***

"She's not nude. She's wearing a—" I stop cold as I get a better look at her. "Cuff her, Granger," I say, holding Fish a little bit tighter.

Georgie's eyes widen my way as she attempts to snatch the puppy from my mother's arms.

"You wouldn't arrest an old lady who's holding a puppy, would you?" she shouts, and another rumble cycles through the crowd.

Santa *ho ho hos* his way over and attempts to remove the sweet pup from her and a rather aggressive tug-of-war ensues.

Fish lets out a hair-raising yowl. **He's not taking my Rudolph back.** She jumps from my arms, and before I know it, she's climbed up the back of Santa's suit and knocked the pointed hat right off his head before making a nest in his snow-white wig.

The poor man does an odd little dance, trying his best to shake the feisty kitty, while Georgie stalks her way through the crowd, holding poor Rudolph like a football. She comes my way, and I rush toward her in an attempt to intercept.

Sherlock jumps up and accidentally launches the tiny pup out of Georgie's hands, and I watch as Rudolph goes flying, much to the horror of everyone in the room.

Leo makes a heroic dive as he catches the tiny pooch mid-flight, before stumbling wildly to the right and left. And in an effort to regain his balance, he knocks down the tallest of the three evergreens in the room, sending glass ornaments flying every which way as they explode like grenades.

Note to self: Purchase plastic ornaments next year. And definitely ixnay on inviting a killer to the party.

The night continues to spin out in a fit of madness, and yet the crowd hasn't thinned out a bit.

I did it, a voice calls out. ***And I'm marking this day down on my calendar. From here on out, I declare it a holiday. Quinn Bennet may have thought he was about to end my life, but I beat him to the punch. He's dead, and I'm about to have the first peaceful night's sleep I've had in months. Sleep tight, you traitorous bastard. Don't let the earthworms bite.***

Whoever killed Quinn Bennet isn't feeling the least bit of remorse, and I'll do whatever it takes to uncover who they are and why they did it.

The killer's peaceful nights are numbered.

Christmas is quickly approaching, and I won't let them get away with murder.

Someone has landed themselves on the naughty list, and I'm going to make sure the only gift they receive this year is a pair of state-issued bracelets.

Quinn Bennet might be dead, but I'll make sure he gets one last gift for Christmas, too.

Justice.

4

"You had them cuff me!"

Georgie shouts as she barges into the Country Cottage Café where Emmie and I sit at the counter noshing on her creamy dreamy peppermint bark.

Georgie's hair is wild and frizzy, and she's wearing a forest green kaftan, a much more comfortable look than that cumbersome wonky quilt she tried to pass off as a dress last night.

Outside the wide-set windows the sky is dark, the Atlantic is churning, and snow is on order at some point in the day. But the magic of December outweighs any gloom the weather can bring as garland covered with twinkle lights outlines every nook and cranny in the brightly lit café.

The café has a black and white theme with wrought iron tables and chairs, which are all filled at the moment with guests from the inn. Both guests and townies alike are welcome to dine at the café and, of course, they're welcome to bring their pets. There's a huge enclosed patio off the back that affords expansive views of the sandy cove. And no matter what time of year, how bitter cold it may be, people can often be found walking the cobbled path that leads to the beach.

"Georgie." I rock Rudolph like a baby while he sits snug in a baby sling hanging from my chest. It's something I use to tote Fish around in, so I thought I'd try it with Rudolph and he really seems to love it. Last night when we got home, he ran laps around my tiny cottage until he was spent and passed out by the fireplace. Seeing that he can't be more than seven or eight weeks old, I thought cradling him might be a good way to start the morning. "I did not have you cuffed," I tell her, taking another bite out of Emmie's melt in your mouth peppermint bark. "Okay, so I may have had you cuffed, but you were naked. What was I supposed to do?"

"I had undergarments on. I was wearing a G-string."

Emmie giggles. "A G-string, Georgie? Really?"

"What's the matter with that? It has my name on it. The G stands for Georgie. It was practically made for me."

"The G stands for groin," I say, petting Fish with my foot as she curls up next to Sherlock Bones at the base of my stool. "But never mind that. What do you have on the agenda today?"

Georgie narrows her left eye as she studies me. "What do *you* got going on, kid? Any plans to rough up the bad guys? Heading to a dive bar to shake up a perp? If you're in, I'm in. I'm your ride or die, and don't you forget that."

My lips pinch tightly. "Okay, so I might be headed off to speak to someone later, but first, I've got to take this little fuzzy bear to the vet and get him checked out."

I omit the tiny detail about meeting both Leo and Huxley at Preston Jewelers. I didn't exactly tell Leo or Huxley that I was working them both just yet. But they're smart boys. They'll figure it out as soon as they see one another sorting through rings.

I still can't believe they're both plotting their matrimonial moves at the very same time, in December no less when my free time has been cut down to nil—not to mention the fact Quinn Bennet was slaughtered right here on the grounds of his most treasured piece of real estate. And how I hate the irony. But nevertheless, I'll move heaven and this inn to help both Leo and Hux give their prospective brides the proposals of their dreams.

Emmie nods. "She's investigating. Where are you off to, Biz?"

I shrug. "I thought I'd start with that woman who sang 'Silent Night.'"

"She was good," Emmie muses. "Is she staying at the inn?"

"*Pfft.*" Georgie takes a seat next to me. "What fun would that be? Here's hoping we find her in some seedy nightclub in Edison where they make women like me dance in cages while men with hairy chests, wearing thick gold chains, throw nickels at us." She looks my way. "I've got a pair of go-go boots that haven't go-goed in a long time. My waist may have expanded, but my feet remain the same. I'll go-go dust 'em off."

Juni enters the café and slogs on over. Her hair is mussed, her mascara is smeared, and she's wearing a fuzzy pink bathrobe.

"Coffee, pancakes, bacon," she mutters to no one in particular.

Sherlock sits up at attention, and Juni gives him a quick scratch.

"Yeah, yeah," she gravels out the words. "Make it extra bacon."

Sherlock gives a cheery bark. *We'll need bacon for Rudolph, too. He's got a long flight ahead of him, and Christmas Eve will be here before we know it.*

Fish mewls, *Oh, for Pete's sake, Sherlock. Jasper was just teasing. Rudolph isn't a reindeer and he's not flying with Santa on the big night. If you don't stop believing in silly things, you'll end up on the naughty list. Naughty dogs don't find bacon in their stocking. They find something called coal. I hear it's not nearly as delicious.*

Sherlock whimpers my way. *Bizzy, please tell me coal tastes like bacon. I can't stand the suspense.*

I shake my head over at him.

"But don't worry. You're a good little doggie," I say, giving his head a scratch. "Once Rudolph leads that flight, you might even find a dinosaur bone under the tree."

Fish groans. *Et tu, Bizzy? You're not making my job any easier.*

Rudolph begins to bark and squirm. *I'd like to try this bacon for myself. And I can't wait to fly through the sky just like I did last night.* He licks my face with a marked enthusiasm. *Who knows? Bacon just might be the key to get me to remember something else from that horrible scene.*

"Right." I laugh as I tilt my head from side to side while he offers up his kisses. "Someone is feeling frisky and he's willing to do and say anything for bacon."

"I'm on it. I'd do anything for that face," Emmie says, quickly disappearing to the back.

"Me too," Georgie howls, giving Rudolph's forehead a quick scratch.

"Me three." Juni dots a kiss to his nose.

"Good," I say as I pull the baby sling off of me and hold Rudolph out toward Georgie and Juni. "Which one of you wants to drop Rudolph off at the vet for me this morning? I'm running late. I told Leo and Hux I'd help them pick out rings because their lucky plus ones are getting a proposal for Christmas."

Georgie's jaw roots to the floor. "Lucky Emmie. Unlucky Hux." She shrugs. "*Eh.* He never was the brightest bulb of the Baker bunch."

I wrinkle my nose. "If Mackenzie says yes, she'll be wife number four."

Juni's chest bucks. "How about that? He's turning out to be a wife collector just like your daddy." She takes Rudolph from me.

"Mmm." I moan through another quick bite of peppermint bark. "That could be the best news I've heard all day. That would mean Mackenzie Woods was just a passing phase."

Someone from behind clears their throat in an obnoxious manner and my shoulders hike as I squeeze my eyes shut.

"Tell me it's not her," I mutter.

"It's her," Mackenzie crows from behind.

Juni snorts out a laugh as she kisses the feisty puppy in her arms. "I'll take the wee one to the vet. I've got to take Sprinkles, too." Sprinkles is Juni's peppy little fur baby she adopted a few months back.

Sherlock barks. ***I'm coming, too! Don't worry, Rudolph. If they try to put the cone of shame on you, I'll bite their toes off.***

Sherlock has yet to forgive me for that.

Rudolph yelps in a panic as Juni and Sherlock head off to find a table.

I turn and smile at the stony-faced brunette before me.

"Mayor Woods." An elastic smile stretches across my face. Mackenzie Woods is the exact reason why I have this little supernatural talent of mine. We were at a Halloween party in our teens and near ground zero for bobbing for apples when Mack decided to shove me into a whiskey barrel filled with water.

Four things happened to me that day. I developed an irrational fear of confined spaces, I'm terrified of immersing myself in a body of water, it kicked off a lifetime distrust of Mackenzie Woods, and last, but never least, I walked away with the ability to pry into other people's minds. I'm transmundane, further classified as telesensual, meaning I have the ability to listen in on other people's private musings. I suppose I've always been transmundane, but Mack's desire to plunge me to the bottom of that barrel and hold me under was the event that awakened those abilities in me. Anyway, she recently revealed that she did it on a dare initiated from my brother. Go figure. Turns out, they've been an evil team from the very beginning.

I lift my chin her way. "What can I do for you?"

"Stop stumbling upon dead bodies, for one." She folds her arms tightly across her cranberry-colored suit. "Really, Bizzy? It's Christmastime."

Georgie scuttles up. "Speaking of which, what's on order for Cider Cove for the big day?"

Mackenzie takes a moment to scowl over at the kaftan lover by my side.

"Not a nude granny," she snips. "You're just as bad as she is."

Georgie scoffs. "I'm an upstanding citizen and soon-to-be business owner in this community. I won't stand by while my own mayor berates me."

"An upstanding citizen?" Mackenzie's brows hike with amusement. "Then act like it." She turns to me. "I was going to ask the Country Cottage Café to cater the appetizers and desserts for the Cider Cove Christmas Spectacular at the end of this month, but seeing that you breed bodies wherever you go, I'm not so sure. You'd think now that you were hitched to that heartthrob, you'd be far more concerned with bringing forth life into this world as opposed to death, but I can see you're still willing to propagate your little deadly hobby."

She's not entirely wrong. In fact, right about now, I'd like to propagate the urge I have to wrap my hands around her skinny little neck. Just for kicks, of course. But I'm not all that interested in having to deal with yet another corpse at the inn.

Instead, I flex a dry smile. "The café will happily provide whatever you need. Just tell us when and where."

"The night before Christmas Eve." Her cheeks flicker as she looks to Georgie. "Be ready for a retail onslaught. The event takes place on Main Street. There will be sleigh rides, Santa, an entire gaggle of annoying little kids, and with Bizzy around, there will most likely be a body." She takes a moment to glower my way. "Try not to make it anyone I know."

"How about you?" Georgie winks. "Care to throw your hat in the ring?"

Mackenzie all but growls at the two of us. "I have to go. I have an early lunch date coming up with a member of the Baker family—one who I happen to find much more tolerable." She stalks off and I turn to Georgie.

"Hey? Maybe Hux has decided to nix the proposal? He can't possibly shop for a ring then speed off to meet Mackenzie."

Georgie smacks me on the arm. "I bet that's it. Boy, you really dodged a sister-in-law bullet. Give me a second to get a Danish to go, and I'll join you at the jewelers."

"Are you sure? Things could get boring fast."

"Are you kidding? The jewelry shop is on the top five list of where to pick up single men."

"Oh, I don't think so."

"Watch and learn, kiddo."

Preston Jewelers is a posh jewelry shop in the downtown district of Seaview and hung right outside their door is a countdown calendar to Christmas to remind all of their customers time is quickly running out.

Georgie, Fish, and I arrive right on time as we enter the glitzy spacious establishment with its sparkling chandeliers up above, deep navy carpeting, matching navy walls, and rows and rows of glass cases filled with shiny baubles that cost more than my cottage and car combined. Not that I own my cottage, but if I did, I'm betting it would still be undervalued compared to the bling they've got under lock and key here.

Fish mewls as she warms my chest. I traded Juni a leash for the kitty sling and decided to bring Fish along for the ride. I've cleared my schedule for the rest of the day, leaving the inn with my trusty employees, but it's not Christmas gifts I'll be hunting down once things wrap up at the jewelers—I'll be hunting down a suspect.

"Hey, good-looking"—Georgie drops her sunglasses a notch as she looks up at one of the security officers standing guard at the door—"whatcha got cookin'?" She bumps her hip to mine. "Did I tell you, or did I *tell* you? This place is a veritable feast of handsome hunks. And it looks to me, I've landed one right out the gate." She winks up at the man clad in uniform. "So are you hitched, or are you single and ready to mingle?"

The older man with a salt and pepper mustache, barrel chest, and sparkling eyes chuckles as he inspects her.

"Mother Goose cut me loose two years ago," he says. "And I've been a fox ready to trot ever since."

"Oh wow," I muse out loud without meaning to. "You know what they say"—I pat her on the back—"every pot has a lid." I glance to my right and spot a handsome homicide detective earnestly inspecting one of the glass shelves and my mouth falls open. "Speaking of lids, I just found mine."

I speed over, and not only do I find Jasper, but Leo and Hux are here, too, each one looking just as dapper as the next.

Jasper wraps his arms around me and offers up a kiss, and the scent of his cologne and his rock-hard wall of a body make me want to pull him off to a dark corner and have my way with him.

"Easy, girl," Leo says, raising a brow my way. He's donned his tan deputy uniform, and I'm guessing he's on a break—not to mention the fact he just read my dirty mind.

I smile up at Jasper. "What are you doing here?"

Fish mewls as if she wanted answers, too.

Hux chuckles. "What do you think he's doing here, Biz? Christmas is coming. He was just picking out something pricey to drop in your stocking."

Jasper glowers at him a moment. "You do realize I'm here to help Leo pick out a ring."

I wink up at him. "Good cover." I give Hux and Leo a quick embrace. "Now let's get down to business. I brought my best girl to help me get to the bottom of this diamond dilemma." I give Fish a quick scratch behind her ears to annunciate my point.

Hux shakes his head. "I'm not going with diamonds."

Fish mewls, **Figures. Mackenzie requires a stone made of blood.**

Leo tips his head. "Should I ditch diamonds?"

"You're going with diamonds, for sure," I tell him before reverting to my brother. "And for you, how about one of those twist tie wires you find on bread packages? I think it's terribly romantic."

Hux frowns my way. "And I think you're a terrible liar. You're making me think I recruited the wrong sister."

I flick my wrist at him. "You got the right sister. If Macy were here, she'd be fighting Georgie to date the security guard. What are you thinking for Mack?" I refrain from suggesting fool's gold.

"White sapphire," he says, nodding at a row of stunning rings set out on the counter.

Jasper dots a finger to one of them. "And they only run a couple hundred bucks."

"Really?" I muse to my brother. "With the way you're snapping up future ex-wives, I think it's the only economical choice. I like this one." I pick up a square cut stone with a halo of mini white sapphires all around it.

Jasper shoots me a look. "You sure? That looks an awful lot like your ring."

I gasp as I look down at my bejeweled hand.

Fish chortles. **Oh goody. You and Mackenzie can be twinsies. I'd be careful not to touch rings, or the two of you are liable to open the portal to the underworld.**

Leo bucks with a laugh. "Fish, you are one smart cat."

I twitch my lips. "On second thought," I say, picking up a silver ring with a teardrop shaped stone. "This is exactly what you should give Mackenzie."

Good thinking. Fish sniffs in the direction of the dainty ring. **There will be tears involved. Let the ring serve as a harbinger.**

I nod. Only too bad my brother won't heed to its warning.

"Great." Hux snaps it up and holds it out to a blonde woman standing behind the counter. "I need this in a size seven. I'll swing by in a week to pick it up."

"That's it?" I balk. "No agonizing, no hemming and hawing? No vacillating and having nightmares over mortgaging your soul in an effort to afford it?"

Hux shoots Leo with his finger. "That would be Granger's job. I'm old hat at this. Besides, who are we kidding? The real prize Mack is getting in this marriage is me." He flashes a cheesy smile. "Gotta run." He pulls me in for another quick hug. "I'm meeting Mack for lunch." **In a hotel room with a bag of burgers. The burgers will be for dessert. Right about now, Mack's my favorite meal.**

"Please get going," I say, giving him a shove as he jets out the door. At least this way I won't have to hear any more about his ravenous appetite.

Leo groans. "TMI. And might I recommend telling your brother about your little talent? He's got a one-track mind."

Jasper inches back as he looks at me. "I thought you said you hear white noise when things get freaky."

"I do," I tell him. "But Hux was walking a fine freaky line."

Leo leans in and studies a couple dozen rings the blonde jeweler has set out on the counter. "I think Hux is right. I'm going to have to mortgage my soul."

"I said that," I correct him as we peruse the glitzy selections. "Don't think about the price. Think about how lovely these will look on Emmie's finger—for the next fifty or seventy years. I know Emmie. She's practical. She'll want to wear it as a wedding ring, too."

Jasper picks up a rectangular emerald cut diamond that makes me drool on sight.

"That would pair nicely with the ring I have now." I hold my hand out flirtatiously. "You're not a secret millionaire, are you?"

Fish brays out an unmistakable laugh. ***The man wanted to cut out my Fancy Beast cat food, Bizzy. A millionaire? I think not.***

Jasper winces. "She's still upset about the cat food, isn't she?"

Leo ticks his head to the side. "You don't come between a girl and her favorite meal."

Fish mewls at Leo, ***I knew I liked you.***

Jasper picks up another ring. "Well, I'm not a millionaire. In fact, I'd better get back to work before they stop signing my paychecks. I think I'll stop by forensics and see how it's going. They're searching the body for foreign material and DNA."

"Sounds exciting," I say with a wry smile. "I can't believe someone had the nerve to kill Quinn at his own event, at his own *inn*. Speaking of the case, I was thinking about it this morning and I couldn't help but note that Arthur was missing last night after the room was cordoned off."

Leo glances to Jasper. "She's right. I didn't see him either."

Jasper's cheek hikes a notch. "That was the guy Quinn introduced as his accounts manager?"

I give a single nod. "I think we should start there first. I bet he had to leave early to dispose of his clothes after he splattered Quinn's blood all over them."

"Then that's where I'll start." Jasper slides the ring back to the counter. "Bizzy, the holidays are here. The inn is bursting at the seams, and more than anything, I want you to be safe. How about as an early Christmas gift, you let me have at this case all by my lonesome?"

"I'll help," Leo is quick to volunteer before he looks at me. "And that will free up more of your time to figure out when and where I should get down on bended knee."

"The *when* will be Christmas Eve; the *where* will be a little trickier to figure out. Hux wants my input, too, but I can assure you Emmie's proposal will be spectacular." I bite down on my lip as I look to Jasper. "How about this, once you track down Arthur to have a word with him, you bring me along? I can read his mind. I'm an invaluable part of your team."

"I can read minds," Leo says, holding up a tiny diamond and I shake my head at it.

"But I'm a woman," I tell them. "I bring out different thoughts in men—lust, greed—both of which could get his wheels churning on why he killed Quinn."

"*If*"—Jasper lands those pale gray eyes over me—"he killed Quinn." He sighs hard. "I'm sorry, Bizzy. Someone came at Quinn Bennet with an axe. They chopped his hand off. This is a ruthless killer. I'd hate to think what they'd do if they knew you were onto them." He wraps his arms around me tightly and Fish peers up at him. "I'll take on Arthur. I've got a good feeling I can wrap this up before Christmas. And that will be my gift to you."

Leo shakes his head. "I wouldn't let him off so easy, Bizzy. He's in a jewelry store. Make up a wish list for him. If my credit card is going to be wounded, so should his."

"No thanks." I wrinkle my nose at Jasper. "Your credit card is my credit card. I'd prefer no part of us wounded come Christmas." I wiggle my wedding ring his way. "I'm good with the bling I've got."

His phone chirps and he digs it out. "Forensics wants to speak with me. I'd better get going. Leo, snap a picture of whatever you chose and shoot it to me. I trust Bizzy." He lands a steamy kiss to my lips. **Rumor has it, Santa might stop by the bedroom tonight. I've got a red pointy hat and**

I'm not afraid to use it. He pulls back and winces at Leo. "Sorry, man. I keep forgetting you can read me like a book."

A dull smile flickers on Leo's lips. "No sweat. See you later. Or should I say *ho ho ho*?"

"Funny." He dots my cheek with a kiss. "Remember, Arthur Silver is off-limits." Jasper gives Fish a quick pat before taking off.

Leo and I search the entire jewelry store before settling on three different rings. The blonde jeweler assisting us suggested we give it some breathing room, so we decide to come back next week.

I collect Georgie at the door and we say goodbye to Leo.

"So where are we off to now, Biz?" Georgie straightens her kaftan, and I can't help but notice her hair is slightly more mussed than usual and her lipstick slightly smeared.

"Georgie, were you getting frisky with that mall cop?"

"He's a man of the badge, Bizzy. And his name is Frodo. I've got his number, and I'm not afraid to use it."

"Well, save it, because right now we need to hunt down a woman by the name of Angelica Chatfield."

Jasper might have said that Arthur Silver was off-limits, but he didn't say a thing about Angelica.

5

Heading to the Lux Eatery.

I shake my head at Angelica Chatfield's Insta Pictures account.

"If I was a stalker, I'd know exactly where she is at all times," I say to Georgie as we get out of the car.

"What fun would that be? I'd find someone else to stalk. I like a good challenge," Georgie says as she lands Rudolph into the leather tote bag I brought along to cart him in.

Fish balked at the idea of heading off to a fancy restaurant to track down an extra fancy socialite and opted to take a nap back at the cottage. So as soon as Juni dropped Rudolph off, we packed him up and headed out to Rolling Oaks, a ritzy town about a half an hour from Cider Cove. In all fairness, Sherlock wanted to come along, too, but he's a bit too bulky to be a purse puppy, so Juni offered to let him play with Sprinkles at her place.

But everyone knows a puppy is a socialite's biggest weakness and perhaps the world's biggest icebreaker. And I'm all for making that blonde bird sing once again. So puppy power it is.

A beat-up red sedan careens into the lot and glides across the snow as it pulls up next to us, sending both Georgie and me diving into the bushes.

"Hey"—Juni shouts as she gets out in haste—"what did I say about starting the fun without me?"

"Never mind that," I say. "Dig us out of the snow." I hold up a hand and she lands both Georgie and me back to our feet. Juni made it clear she was all about suspects and fine dining, so here she is.

I look up at the ritzy glass building with its gold and marble accents.

Juni grunts as she cranes her neck to get a peek inside. "I bet they've got steak served twelve juicy ways till Sunday."

Georgie rubs her belly. "I'm a traditional Maine girl. Steak and lobster, please—and don't forget to throw in the chowder. And none of that fake Manhattan stuff. If I see a drop of tomato sauce, there will be blood in the water."

Rudolph barks. ***And I want bacon!***

"Great." I give him a quick pat. "We've got another bacon addict on our hands. I see Sherlock's job is done. Let's get in before we turn into snowmen."

We head inside where they check our coats, and thankfully so. It's warm and toasty, decorated to the nines in gold and white Christmas ornaments, not a sign of an evergreen, but it's so gorgeous a part of me wants to emulate the impeccable style next year at the inn.

I glance over at Georgie, and a breath hitches in my throat.

"Georgie, you look amazing," I say, marveling at her green and red tie-dye kaftan. "You should sell these in your shop."

"Are you kidding?" Georgie snarls. "That battle axe of a mother you've got has instated a uniform, and this ain't it."

"Things are going that good, huh? Have you thought of a name yet?"

"Yup"—Juni answers for her—"I came up with it for them last night. The Hippie and the Battle Axe."

I can't help but laugh at that one.

"Table for three?" The older man dressed in a tuxedo bows low as he asks the question, but I'm too busy trying to spot my mark.

"Actually, I was looking for someone—Angelica Chatfield?"

"Oh?" He straightens. "I didn't realize you were with the party. Right this way."

I don't dare correct him as he strides us across the glossy white marble floors, and we bypass well-polished men and women with tiny little meals sitting on their plates—and oddly I've yet to see a single person take a bite. Go figure. I take it the rich don't eat. I knew they weren't like the rest of us, but this little revelation makes me wonder if this planet underwent an alien invasion without knowing it. Wealthy *aliens* who don't need food to fuel their bodies.

The waiter stops short at an oblong table filled with blonde cackling women, all of them ultra-thin, all of them undergoing varying degrees of facial paralysis.

I spot Angelica near the end of the table with a few empty seats around her, and we quickly trot on over and take a seat. Angelica's blonde hair sits in a nest on top of her head, her dark, thick-framed glasses are firmly in place, and she's wearing a fitted red leather jacket over a gold turtleneck.

Not a single woman bats a false eyelash our way as they continue to henpeck one another at a frenetic pace.

Juni and Georgie peruse their menus.

Georgie grunts, "There's not a single price tag on here."

Juni bounces in her seat. "It's our lucky day, Mama. That must mean the food is free."

"It's not free," I whisper just as Rudolph lets out a sharp bark. He looks adorable with his head poking out of my leather bag with that perky smile of his and that bright red ribbon tied onto his matching red collar.

In less than five seconds, every eye is feasted this way as the women all coo collectively in this direction.

A blonde in a shimmering silver top trots over and plucks him out of my bag, and soon enough they're all fighting over him. Lucky for Rudolph, he doesn't seem to mind. He's licking up every frozen face he comes across.

"Say." Angelica taps me on the arm. "Isn't that the dog from last night?" Her poinsettia red lips round out as she takes me in. "And aren't you the beekeeper I met?" She casually holds up her wine glass, and a sommelier appears from out of nowhere to fill it.

Georgie leans in and whispers, "She's tipsy, Biz. Pump a little more truth serum into her, and we'll have the case solved before the appetizers arrive."

Here's hoping.

"I'm an innkeeper, actually." I offer a warm laugh. "I'm Bizzy. We met just before you went on. And these are my friends, Georgie and Juni." I nod at her. "And by the way, your performance was amazing."

"Thank you." She gives a few rapid blinks. "I guess you can say I'm pleased with the way things turned out last night."

Juni kicks me from under the table and makes a face.

I know, right? I nod back at her.

How could Angelica be pleased with the way things turned out last night—unless, of course, she's the killer.

"I thought the performances were outstanding." That's the truth. If it weren't for that little dismembering detail, the night would have been perfect. "Do you perform regularly?"

Angelica is quick to wave it off. "I don't have time for that." She winks at someone down at the other end of the table. "I'm a woman of the world. I'm far too busy with the galas, the endless shopping for all the *it* parties I'm to attend."

"That's—lovely." I force a smile to come and go.

"No, it's not lovely." She laughs at the thought. **It's dog eat dog is what it is. Just maintaining this lifestyle is enough to make me want to crawl under the covers and stay there. I'd much rather be home with a good book by the fire than at this table full of ninnies, but duty calls.** She shrugs. "Some days are better than others." **It'll be hard to top last night, but like they say on Broadway, the show must go on.**

I lean in and wince. "I'm sorry to ask, but did you know Quinn Bennet well?"

Her eyes close a moment. "Too well." Her expression sours at the mention of him. "Quinn and I dated off and on. He was a playboy, you know. I was just one woman in that harem he kept. I knew the rules and played along." Her eyes flit to the side when she says that last part.

A waitress comes over to take our orders, and Juni raises her hand in haste.

"Escrow Gots!" She elbows her moody mother. "That's fancy speak for land lobsters."

I shake my head at her. "Actually, I'm pretty sure it's a funny way to say snails."

"Ha!" Juni lifts her wine glass my way, already brimming with the red stuff. "Look at Ms. Fancy Pants ready and willing to pull one over on me." She snaps her fingers at the waitress. "Make it two orders. I came ready to play." She pats her stomach and winks at me.

Great. Good thing my credit card came ready to play, too. But I'd much rather have a bauble from Prestons for what this is going to cost me.

Georgie orders the clam chowder, and I do the same. The rest of the table rattles off a number to her, and she seems to know what that means before taking off.

Angelica tries to angle in toward the conversation going on to her left, and I scoot my chair next to hers another inch.

"So did you get to reconnect with Quinn before he was—you know?" I can't bring myself to say the word *murdered*.

"Oh yes, I saw him"—her brows flex a moment—"right before the show." *I told that handsome officer last night that I didn't speak to Quinn after he left the stage. I'd better stick to the story. The murder happened at the inn. This poor girl probably hasn't been shaken down by the sheriff's department just yet, and she looks darn right fragile. I bet she'll sing like a canary as soon as they ask her what her name is. No, I'd better keep the details of our last meeting to myself.*

Okay, fine. My lips twitch side to side. Two can play at that game. And one of them can play really well, especially when she has the advantage to read her opponent's mind.

"Before the show?" I tip my head her way. "I hope you enjoyed the hot cocoa and sweet treats that were laid out." Because I happened to see her doing both—right before she landed something toxic into Quinn's drink. Come to think of it, I forgot to mention it to Jasper. I'll make sure he runs Quinn's blood work.

Angelica gurgles out a laugh. "Oh, I had those delicious cookies before and after the show. And that peppermint bark?" She rolls her eyes to the ceiling. "I hope you don't think less of me, but I not only had my fair share, I brought a small plate home with me, too." ***And that's exactly how I celebrated.***

Celebrated?

She leans in. "So is everything set for the reading of the will?"

"The reading of the *will*?" My eyes bulge in disbelief. The man hasn't been dead for twenty-four hours and already the vultures are circling.

Georgie taps her knee to mine. "Boy, the rich don't waste time, do they? Hey? Do you think it's too late for me to get in on that action?"

Angelica belts out a laugh, and Rudolph gives a happy bark from across the way as the women continue to vie for his adorable affection.

I love it here, Bizzy! I never want to leave. No sooner does he shoot the thought my way than the socialite that's holding him helps him lap the water out of her crystal goblet.

Angelica leans toward Georgie. "You're not the only one asking if it's too late to get in on the action. And believe me, the shroud of mystery around this thing is driving my friends bonkers. I spoke to Quinn's lawyer last night. It looks as if the reading is taking place in the library at the inn. He still needs to shore up some details, but that's the way Quinn wanted it done when the time came." ***And lucky for me, the time came last night, right around nine o'clock.***

I don't even know how to process all that information.

Lucky for her?

She called his *lawyer* last night?

"The reading of the will is taking place at the inn?" I say that last bit out loud before taking a sip of my water.

"Oh yes." Angelica dabs her lips with a pristine white cloth and leaves a lip stain on it. "Right after the séance."

I nearly shoot the water out of my nose.

"A séance! A séance!" Juni jumps up and down in her seat, and for some reason, the rest of the socialites follow her lead. Good Lord, it's as if they've finally found their leader. And, they might have a heck of a lot more fun if Juni were leading the charge. For starters, there would be land lobsters for everyone.

"No to the séance." I shake my head at Juni. "That is not happening at the inn. It's Christmastime, for Pete's sake."

"That's right." Georgie smacks her hand down over the table. "If they want to host that dark perversion, they'll have to come up to my place. What I wouldn't do to have a hot dead ghost like Quinn Bennet haunting my halls. Meow." She claws at the air, and I can't help but groan.

"No to that, too," I say in the event Angelica decides to take her up on it.

Angelica makes a face my way. "Okay, have it your way. Who wants him there, anyway?" **Spewing who knows what.** She averts her eyes once again, and I'm getting the feeling Angelica very much prefers that Quinn keeps his ghostly trap shut.

On second thought, maybe I shouldn't have ixnayed the idea so quickly.

Lunch arrives, and sure enough, each woman has a large white platter set in front of them with what amounts to a handful of lawn clippings and a side of sliced radish. Both Georgie and I have a shot-glass worth of clam chowder, and Juni, well, her meal takes the cake. And I'm betting she's wishing she went for the cake instead.

Juni's dual order of escargot consists of two oversized snails that look as if they're about to rumble—albeit very slowly.

"What in the fresh hell is this?" Juni backs her seat up a notch as if she were afraid they were about to attack.

Angelica laughs. "You're my people, Juni." ***Lord knows people like Juni are kinder and far more genuine than the vipers I run with. I should know. I've been running with the likes of Juni for years now and loving every manic minute of it.*** "Here." She slides her lawn clippings over to Juni. "Let's see if the snails are hungry."

The four of us break out into a fit of laughter, causing the rest of the table to pause from their own zombie-like cackling.

Lunch begins to wind down, and I can feel my access to Angelica beginning to winnow away. It's time to be bold.

"Can I ask you a question?" I shrug over at the friendly blonde. "Who do you think could have done something like that to poor Quinn?"

She swallows hard. The muscles in her jaw tighten as she grows stiff.

And sadly, not a single thought flits through her mind.

"Eve." She nods as if she were trying to convince herself. "Eve French. She wanted Quinn to herself in the worst way. She was his number one for many years, but she just couldn't stand sharing him. And unfortunately, that's the way the wealthy cookie crumbled, and because of it, they crumbled, too. But it wasn't Eve who broke things off. Quinn felt as if her constant need for monogamy was wearing him down, so he went to England to think." She shrugs. "We all know how that turned out. He stayed for years. And Eve grew bitter. She married for a while, and the man turned out to be a cad as well—a conniving one at that. He gambled away her fortune. Eve was a trust fund baby. And from what I hear, she hardly has two dimes to rub together these days. Oh, she has that shop of hers, but that's about it."

"That's terrible," I say. "I met her daughter last night. She was very sweet."

"She's precocious is what she is. She takes after her mother. The paternity was in question for a while, but boy, was she fuming when she found out the kid didn't belong to Quinn. She wanted to anchor herself to that big pile of money he had. But she did marry the kid's father. He was the aforementioned gambling louse."

"But why would any of that drive Eve to bury an axe into the man's chest?"

Angelica shudders as if reliving a very bad memory.

"Actually"—she glances over her shoulder before leaning my way—"it would. You see, Eve blames Quinn for her downfall. And I have no doubt she not only wanted him back last night—she wanted to *get* him back. That axe was a prop from the play." She shakes her head at me. "That wasn't premeditated. It was an act of passion, and no one felt more passionate last night than Eve." **And perhaps me, but I'm not giving that away for free. Nope. That little passionate tidbit is just for me.**

And me.

Lunch wraps up, and the socialites take off as if the table were on fire.

Soon, it's just Angelica left holding the bag, or the cute little puppy as it were.

"Would you mind?" She hands Rudolph over to me with his smiling face and frenetically wagging tail. "I've got to powder my nose." She makes a run for the front door, and we see her speeding off into the snowy afternoon.

"Hey!" Georgie calls after her. "The restroom is that way." She hitches a thumb behind her just as the waitress places something in her hand. "What's this?" Georgie pulls the slim black leather case forward. "How do you like that? I think I get a purse out of the deal."

"That's the check," I say, taking it from her and opening it up. "Oh my goodness. This can't be right." I glance up at the blonde waitress hovering above on standby. "Has this been paid?"

"It will be." She offers a stern look my way.

I fork over my credit card and watch as all the money I've saved to do my Christmas shopping with—for the next *two* years—does a disappearing act.

Someone may have iced Quinn Bennet, but I have feeling I was just frosted by a gaggle of socialites.

6

Main Street is covered in a blanket of white sparkling fluff that gives Cider Cove all the magic a month like December demands. The lampposts are wrapped in garland and twinkle lights, and each one is dotted with an enormous red velvet bow. The entire town looks as if it's out of a storybook, and a part of me wishes we could leave the decorations up all year long.

Georgie asked to be dropped off at her new store, so I park and Rudolph and I head in with her. As soon as we step inside the dusty shop cluttered with boxes, Mom drops the broom she's holding and dashes our way.

"Give me that baby!" She shuffles over in her slippers and a red bandana wrapped around her head. "I've just *broken* myself today." She groans as she takes Rudolph from me and he proceeds to lick her face silly.

Macy comes up from behind with her hair neatly combed, wearing a festive red sweater dress paired with long black boots.

"I'm not lifting a finger around here." She steals Rudolph from my mother. "I'm simply checking out the competition." She holds Rudolph out a notch and examines the fun-loving, smiling pup. "Hey, you're pretty cute." She nods my way. "Why don't you let me have him for a few hours? I bet he could double my sales." Macy's shop, Lather and Light, is located exactly across the street and has never been short of customers, especially not this time of year.

My sister isn't exactly what I would call an animal lover, but I see she has no problem profiting off their adorable looks. Can't say I blame her. Rudolph has the ability to brighten anyone's day and is apparently wildly adored by socialites and common folk alike. I'm betting she's onto something with that whole fiscal increase she's sure his furry features will bring.

"Sorry," I tell her. "Puppy labor laws prohibit him from working more than his concentration will allow. And seeing that's about two minutes, I'm afraid no can do."

I take a quick look around. The shop is rectangular in nature, with large bay windows set in front, rustic wood floors, and a register that sits on a long counter situated in the back. Last month there were nefarious things happening right here in this very store, but now with the killer behind bars, and with Georgie and my mother at the helm, I think they're about to give this place the cheerful resurrection it deserves.

Georgie rips open a small box and begins pulling out one wonky quilt after another, far more than that tiny box looks like it could hold to begin with. Each quilt was handcrafted by whatever senior guild Georgie was able to bamboozle into doing her dirty work this month. And each one is alive with both vibrant colors and buzzing patterns.

"Come on, Toots." Georgie motions my mother over. "Don't just stand there growing old. We've got inventory to offload. We want to get this hovel open by Christmas, don't we?"

Mom shoots her a look. "Who are you calling old?" She makes her way over with a groan. "And I've been thinking we need to expand our inventory. You *know*, in case someone strolls in and they don't need a quilt. I say we keep a few candles on hand. In fact, I've got two boxes sitting right over there."

Macy clears her throat. "How quickly you forget I had to put out a hit on the last girl who opened a candle shop here just last month."

"Not funny." I groan. "In fact, don't even think about repeating those words outside these doors. The people of this town are going to hate you."

"They're going to *fear* me," she corrects with a saccharin smile. "But I'm open to hate, too. I've never felt the need for people to like me. Unlike you, Bizzy."

"I don't need anyone to like me either." Okay, so maybe I do, but just a little. "And you did not put a hit out on anyone.

The poor thing was murdered. Besides, her killer is behind bars, and this shop is about to take on new life with whatever Mom and Georgie have planned."

Mom scoffs as she looks over at Georgie. "What *do* we have planned? I have to order the signage this afternoon if we want to have that grand opening in a week. We need a name for this place, and we need it fast."

"I've got one," Macy says as she sets Rudolph down and he runs a spastic lap around the shop, barking and jumping with all the joy a puppy can muster. "How about Hags R Us?"

Georgie frowns over at her. "Don't make me wave the special finger at you."

Rudolph runs over to her. ***Does the special finger have bacon? Wave the special finger at me, Georgie! Wave it! Wave it!***

She digs into her pocket and tosses him a handful of crispy pork fat, and all is well in puppy land.

"No hags." Mom blows out a breath. "We need something serious. Something that makes people want to do business with us."

"Serious?" Macy grunts as Rudolph kicks a piece of bacon near her leather boots. "How about Lady and the Tramp?"

Mom gives a husky laugh. "Hear that, Georgie? She just called you a tramp." She winks my way when she says it.

Georgie waves her off. "Everyone knows the tramps are much more fun. How about Good Time Granny and Buzzkill

Betty? We can make a game of it and let the customers guess which is which."

Macy chortles. "The reason you can't decide on a name is because you don't have a focus. Look at all this junk. You've got quilts, dresses made from quilts, candles—which you probably stole from me. What's next? Sandwiches?"

"Sandwiches!" Georgie snaps her fingers and dances as if she just scored the winning touchdown at the Super Bowl. "I vote for hot pastrami."

Mom rolls her eyes. "Do you see what I'm up against?"

I head over and grab one of the wonky quilt dresses Georgie is laying out over a glossy wooden table.

"These are kind of fun," I say, holding it up on front of me. It's primarily comprised of green and white gingham fabric with a few prints of Santa on a snowy roof and a few reindeer in the mix. "I can wear it around the cottage."

"Oh, Bizzy." Macy looks visibly ill as she inspects me with it against my body. "I had no idea you were already looking to get out of that booby trap of a marriage you landed in."

"Funny," I say as I frown over at her.

"She's right." Mom tosses her hands in the air. "Wear that around the house and Jasper will divorce you in a week."

"Mother, he would not. Jasper wouldn't care if I walked around in a garbage bag."

"You're getting close," Macy mutters.

Georgie snaps her fingers. "Then that's how we'll market them. Want to give the old man his walking papers? Parade around in this beauty, and you'll have full control of the remote *and* your finances within a week. Guaranteed or your money back."

Mom groans ten times harder than before—right before she straightens with a jolt.

"Wait a minute!" She tips her head toward Georgie. "I think you may be onto something. We should have a silly sales magnet that offers women of a certain age something they need. Something to make them feel powerful and independent like they don't need a man."

Macy lifts her chin. "Just for the record, I call dibs on battery-operated boyfriends."

"What?" Mom balks as she waves her off. "No. I don't mean that. And you shouldn't either." She wags a finger at her oldest daughter. "I think we should sell things that speak to the soul of the more mature woman."

"Like Tom Selleck?" Georgie picks up Rudolph as she steps our way.

"No." Mom squeezes her eyes shut with exasperation. "Not like Tom Selleck. Like something you want to cuddle up with by the fire."

Georgie nods. "Tom Selleck."

"Mom"—I shrug over at her—"I hate to point out the obvious, but that's what you've got the quilts for. How about marketing the store as something in keeping with the theme? You can call it something like Cozy Corner, or Me Time, or Get Bundled."

Mom gasps. "That's great! And we can have a monthly book selection to go along with it. In fact, we can have a book club."

"Oh!" Georgie raises her hand. "We can sell those pinecones that turn colors when you toss them into the fire, and tea, coffee, and some of that peppermint bark from the Cottage Café."

Mom taps a finger to her temple. "Now you're thinking."

"And kaftans!" Georgie plucks a red kaftan out of a box and waves it like a harbinger of hostile things to come—namely tie-dye kaftans. "Bizzy, you put on one of these around the house and you'll have Jasper for life."

Macy squints over at her. "How do you figure?"

"Easy access," Georgie says without missing a beat. "Come to think of it, same with the wonky quilt dress. Now there's a feature worth highlighting."

My phone buzzes in my hand before I can respond to her, and it's a text from the man I'm looking to give easy access to himself, Jasper.

Just got home. Picked up dinner. Bad news. It looks as if someone stole our credit card and spent over 1K this afternoon. Don't worry. I shut down the card.

A breath gets locked in my throat.

"I'd better get home. Jasper is there." I stretch my lips back as I look to Georgie. "I'll give you twenty bucks for that kaftan."

Georgie tosses it my way. "And just like that, we've got our first customer!"

I do a quick change, scoop up Rudolph, and head back to my cottage.

Here's hoping a little easy access will make Jasper forget all about my poor purchasing decisions.

The cottage I share with Jasper was once exclusively mine. Jasper rented the cottage next door, but when we got hitched a few months back, we consolidated into this one. They're both on the grounds of the inn and within walking distance to work for me, which I love. Emmie, Jordy, and Georgie live on the grounds as well. If I could, I'd move everyone I love here.

Jasper and I spent last weekend decorating the outside of our cozy little cottage with a wreath made of evergreen boughs, colorful twinkle lights to line the roof, and we set poinsettias on either side of the entrance to give it an extra festive touch.

I let myself in, only to find the fireplace roaring, the living room toasty, and Fish and Sherlock curled up on the sofa. The inside of the cottage has a cozy appeal, too, with its yellow and white checkered sofa, its frilly curtains, and rustic coffee table.

Jasper and I put up Christmas stockings over the fireplace with our names on them, and there's one each for Fish and Sherlock, too. We put twinkle lights and garland over the mantel and a giant wreath made of holly berries up above the fireplace, but we've yet to get a tree.

"Hey, beautiful." Jasper steps out of the kitchen with a couple of plates in one hand and a brown paper bag in the other, looking like the handsome detective he is—a handsome detective who is about to winnow out the truth about that pricey lunch date I had with a *suspect*, of all people.

So I do the only thing I can think of. I set Rudolph down and peel off my coat, dropping it right to the floor as if I was doing a strip tease.

He tips his head back a notch as if to get a better look at me before landing the plates and bag on the coffee table.

"I see you're channeling your inner Georgie," he muses as he wraps his arms around me. "And boy, do I ever approve." Jasper lands a molten hot kiss over my lips, and for a moment, I forget all about the one thousand ways I've managed to land myself in financial hot water. He pulls back. "I hope you don't mind, I picked up a couple of hot pastrami sandwiches for dinner."

I lift a brow. "It sounds as if *you're* channeling your inner Georgie, too." I fill him in on Georgie's hot pastrami sales pitch and we share a warm laugh.

"Sounds delicious," he says, navigating us to the sofa as both Fish and Sherlock hop off and begin to chase Rudolph around the living room in a dizzying circle. "So what happened to your clothes today?" It's clear Jasper isn't buying my kaftan revolution so easily. He looks at me intently and manages to send my stomach searing with heat because Jasper Wilder just so happens to be unfairly handsome. "Why do I get the feeling I'm going to regret asking that question?"

"Would you believe I opted for a stunning frock because it provided something special just for you?"

His brows furrow. "What's that?"

"Easy access." I blink a quick smile "*And*—my purchase of this little ditty allowed me to become the very first customer for my mother and Georgie. So I was essentially doing a very good deed."

"Easy access?" He gets a drugged look in his eyes. "I like where this is headed." He wraps an arm around me and pulls me close. "Are we skipping dinner?"

"Only if you lose your appetite."

A dark laugh brews in his chest. "There's no hope of that happening with you around."

"Oh, I'd say there's a little hope." I cringe at the thought of what comes next. "About that credit card…"

"Don't worry about it." He glances to the ceiling with a look of frustration. "Thank goodness fraud alert kicked in and we were able to squash it. What moron would pay a thousand dollars for lunch? Apparently, someone got ahold of our number and threw a party with it at some ridiculous place out in Rolling Oaks. Can you imagine? I bet they called two hundred of their closest friends and said the words *free lunch*."

"You would be surprised." A nervous laugh trickles out of me. "There weren't *that* many people there."

A laugh initiates from him but quickly diminishes.

"Bizzy?" He backs away a notch. "Tell me you didn't have lunch in Rolling Oaks with two hundred of your closest friends."

"Oh, I didn't. There were only about twelve people there, and not one of them was a friend—unless, of course, you count Georgie and Juni. Would you call them friends? I'm thinking they're more like family."

His eyes widen about as far as they can go. "I call them trouble. Talk fast, Bizzy. I'm filling in the blanks, and I don't like where the pieces are falling."

"Fine." I tell him about how effortless it was to track down Angelica Chatfield and how Georgie, Juni, and I just sat right down at their table and started chatting away.

Jasper tips his head back until all I can see is his Adam's apple.

"Bizzy." He groans. "I guess I should have talked to you first before I spent an hour with the fraud department."

"I'm sorry. If it makes you feel better, I'll call them first thing in the morning and have the charges put back on the card."

His cheek flickers. "It's the right thing to do. I'll take care of it, though. It's the least *I* can do while you're out there chasing the bad guys." He dips his chin, his brows narrowing like a couple of birds in flight. "Bizzy, I asked you earlier to please let me take this case."

"You asked me to keep away from Arthur Silver. And I did. You didn't say anything about Angelica. Besides, she's a woman. I could take her if I had to."

"Could you take a bullet to the heart?"

"You don't fight fair."

"Neither do bullets." He sighs as he washes his gaze over me. "Okay, I give. I get it. Quinn was your boss. This was his inn. This is personal. I'll let you assist. But for the record, *you* are assisting *me*."

"I'm in." I raise my right hand as if I were taking an oath. "I solemnly swear to fully cooperate with your investigation, Detective."

"Who are we kidding?" The hint of a mournful smile appears on his face. "I'm going to be cooperating with *your* investigation. Just don't tell my boss. So what did you glean?"

"Okay, so I still don't know what she dumped in his drink last night."

"You saw her dump something in his drink?"

I nod. "Before the show."

He pulls out his phone. "Making a note to send to forensics."

"I meant to tell you that, but things kept going sideways."

"That is their favorite direction," he says, plopping his phone back onto the table. "And by the way, your investigation is moving too fast." His brows bounce, and although there's a dash of sarcasm in his tone, I know he means it. "What happened at lunch?"

"Angelica was dicey. She lied to me when I asked if she spoke to Quinn after the show. She was about to admit it but then backtracked, thinking she should keep her story consistent with what she told the deputies. But Angelica did admit out loud to calling Quinn's estate attorney last night, wanting to know when they'd have the reading of the will. We're hosting it at the inn, by the way."

"Wow." He gives a wistful shake of the head. "She ran home and called his attorney? It takes a special person to pull a stunt like that. But does it take a killer?"

"Not according to Angelica. She thinks Eve is the axe wielding maniac in this equation."

"Eve French, the jilted girlfriend. I spoke with a few people who told me a little about the relationship she had with Quinn. Spoiler alert: it wasn't a good one."

"That's basically what Angelica said. Oh, and there was one more thing she said that I thought was funny, and it had nothing to do with the case. She mentioned it was exhausting maintaining her lifestyle. I guess there are first-world problems and then there are socialite problems."

Rudolph comes up barking a happy little *yip-yip-yip* while dancing on his hind legs, so I pull him onto my lap.

Fish strides over looking worn out. ***Good idea, Bizzy,*** she mewls. ***Hold him hostage. He's a terror. He's got far too much energy, and it never seems to end.***

I can't help but laugh as I translate to Jasper.

Sherlock moans as he collapses in a heap by the fireplace. ***I don't even care about bacon anymore. I just need naps.*** He closes his eyes, and he's out like a light.

Rudolph bounces between my lap and Jasper's as his wagging tongue and tail all move frenetically along with him.

Those women at the restaurant were talking about the blonde you were with. He vocalizes as if trying to speak the words in perfect English.

"The women were talking about, Angelica?" I lean in. "What were they saying?"

Rudolph gives a sharp bark. ***They said she was broke, and that she had no money. One of them said she probably killed Quinn because she knew she was in the will.***

I glance to Jasper and quickly tell him what I've just learned.

"Hearsay. Gossip at best," he says the words slowly. "But maybe that's what she meant by it's exhausting to maintain the lifestyle? Maybe she *is* broke and she's just keeping up appearances?"

My mouth falls open. "Come to think of it, she said she much prefers to hang out with people like Juni. Maybe she's living a double life? Juni is anything but a socialite."

Jasper nods. "And maybe that's why she stiffed you with the bill."

Fish yowls, *I knew I should have gone along. Point her out to me, Bizzy.* She flicks a claw from her paw. *I'll give her a gift she'll remember for quite some time.*

Rudolph wiggles free and jumps to the floor, giving chase to Fish while barking up a storm.

"The kids are wild tonight." Jasper's lids hood over. "How about if Mom and Dad hit the bedroom early?"

"What about your hot pastrami dinner?"

"Don't tell Santa, but I'm a dessert first kind of a guy. Besides, I've got an access issue to check out for you. I'd hate to think you got ripped off twice in one day."

"Smooth, Wilder, smooth."

He takes me by the hand and we put the kaftan to the test.

Suffice it to say, Georgie wasn't wrong.

7

I think I like donuts better than bacon. Rudolph barks as he makes quick work of the sugary confection that fell to the ground.

Fish gives a long blink. ***For goodness' sake, we've got another monster with the munchies. You've trained him well, Sherlock***, she mewls. ***Your wicked work is done.***

Sherlock barks. ***You're wrong. There's still plenty of work to be done. Nothing is better than bacon.***

It's the middle of the day and the foot traffic at the front desk of the Country Cottage Inn has been comparable to a clearance sale the day after Christmas. It turns out, a bed and breakfast up the way flooded, and we're receiving their current bookings along with their prospective bookings, too.

Thankfully, I've got both of my trusty front desk clerks with me. Nessa Crosby, a feisty brunette who also happens to be a cousin of Emmie's, and Grady Pennington, a real looker with dark hair and far too much Irish charm handed down via his DNA. The girls never fail to swoon in his direction. Both Nessa and Grady came to work at the inn right out of college.

Grady pretends to drop another donut, and this time both Sherlock and Rudolph dive for it at once and a growling fest ensues.

"Grady." I shoot him a look.

"What?" he asks with a laugh caught in his throat. "They're plain donuts. Humans don't like those. They're practically dog food to begin with."

"The point is, they're not dog food. And Rudolph has already informed me he's a donut fanatic."

Nessa moans as she pulls a pink cruller off the platter Emmie dropped off a while ago, along with a basket of her peppermint bark. Initially, I had Emmie bring them for the guests, but Nessa, Grady, and I haven't been able to keep our hands off them.

Who could blame us? It's freezing outside, Christmas is swooping in at supersonic speeds, the guests are cranky, *we're* cranky, and the only thing we want to fuel our bodies with is deep-fried confections and peppermint bark—and coffee, lots and lots of coffee.

"I'm a donut fanatic, too, Rudolph." Nessa reaches down and gives him a pat. "If Bizzy ever tries to withhold a sweet treat, you just find me."

Grady nods my way. "So what's going on with the inn? Is it being sold off? Are we losing our jobs?"

A small wailing sound comes from Nessa. "I can't lose my job at Christmas, Bizzy. Who's going to pay my credit cards off come January? I'll lose my apartment. I'll lose my car. Peanut and I will be homeless and *carless, too*." Peanut is the cute little puppy she adopted last year. It just so happens that his owner was murdered right here at the inn, but that case was solved, and I have no doubt this one will be, too. She takes another bite of her cruller. "Who knew when they hacked Quinn Bennet to pieces they hacked my life to pieces, too?"

"He wasn't hacked to pieces." I wince because she's not entirely wrong. "And would you keep it down? I don't want to freak the guests out." I glance out at the festive garland and red bows dotting the railing that lead to the second story, and my heart aches at the thought of the inn being sold off, but I really don't see another way. "I don't know what's going to happen to the inn, but I guess we'll know soon enough. As for now, it's business as usual."

Until the rug is ripped out from under us.

And the way my luck has been as of late, that should take place in about five hot minutes.

A tall, broad-chested man in a dark coat steps into the foyer and makes his way over, and I recognize that scraggly beard and those twinkling eyes.

"Warwick." I slide off my stool and offer him a cheery grin. "Nice to see you again. What brings you around this afternoon?"

"Nice to see you again, Bizzy." He gives Fish a quick scratch behind her ears, and one of her hind legs thumps with delight. "Looks as if I've hit the sweet spot." He gives a husky laugh. "I was just stopping by to let you know I was contacted by the estate lawyer. It was Quinn's request to hold the reading of the will here in the library. The attorney wanted to schedule it for this Monday at two in the afternoon if that works for you. I told him I'd stop by and ask."

"That's fine. I'll have refreshments and some snacks available. I'm sure a meeting like that can be tense."

He tips his head. "It will be. You have a formal invitation from the attorney. I'm sure Quinn wanted you to be apprised of everything from start to finish. Especially the fate of the inn."

"Thank you. I'll be glad to be there. I'm on pins and needles just waiting to see what he has planned for this place."

Warwick balls up his lips. "I have a feeling he'll have it absorbed into his real estate holdings." He sheds what appears to be a manufactured smile. "You'll be fine." ***A little overhaul, and this dingy old inn will be a modern*** *oasis. We'll have every socialite in Manhattan clamoring to have a room here.*

I take in a breath and hold it.

A modern oasis? What's wrong with having a quaint little inn? And I take umbrage with that dingy remark. I work tirelessly to make sure this place is clean as a whistle.

"Warwick, who do you think will take possession of the inn if it's absorbed into his real estate holdings? A board?"

"No stuffy board. I'm sure whoever it will be, they'll be just as excited about this property as you are." *And I am. I'll have this place producing twice the income.* He gives a sly smile. "If you don't mind, I'd like to have a look around. I haven't been here in years, and the other night, well, I didn't see much but the ballroom and the garden."

"Absolutely. Would you like a tour? I can call the grounds manager, Jordy. He knows every nuance of this inn."

"No, no, that won't be necessary. I'd like a moment to reflect and think of Quinn. Sort of my way of paying my respects."

"I completely understand."

He takes off, and I watch him as he leaves.

Fish stands and lashes her tail my way. *What is it, Bizzy? Why are you looking at him that way? Is he the killer?*

"No, not that," I whisper as I pick her up and kiss her. "But I get the feeling he might be the new owner of the inn." A hard sigh expels from me. "Let's hope I can convince him we can increase the revenue without turning this place into a steel and glass modern monster."

A slew of new guests head in, and both Nessa and Grady tend to them. And on their heels is a feisty blonde in a fitted red peacoat storming my way.

"Hey, Macy," I say. "Are you ready to rock and roll?"

I thought I'd do a little Christmas shopping out in Rose Glen this afternoon at an exclusive little shop called Elora's Closet. I don't see how Jasper could possibly object to that.

"Yes siree." She leans in and lands a kiss to Fish's forehead. "I'm ready and willing to check out my competition." She needles me with her pale blue eyes. "But I'm not willing to watch you interrogate a suspect." She smears a short-lived smile my way. "I know what you're up to. Eve is my friend, Bizzy. She's not a killer. So don't go trying to see if an axe fits in her hand, or whatever it is you're up to. This is strictly shopping. And—I want to see what her holiday inventory looks like. I need to step up my game if I don't want Mom and Georgie to swoop in and steal my lunch."

"I hardly think they're going to steal your lunch."

Sherlock lets out a quick bark. **Speaking of which, I'm starving. How about we make a detour to the kitchen? I bet Emmie has a few burgers lying around. I feel like stealing Emmie's lunch.**

Emmie quite literally had a few burgers lying around last night, when Sherlock spotted them and proved to be a burger-eating magician. One second they were on a platter, the next they were in his stomach.

"How about I feed you lunch back at the cottage?" I pick up Rudolph as his tail wags back and forth like a spring. "Nessa, Grady? I'll be back early this evening. If you need anything at all, give me call."

Fish belts out a crystal clear meow. *What about me?*

"Don't you worry." Macy scoops the furry cutie off the counter as if she understood the sweet cat and plops her into the black leather tote bag cinched to her shoulder. Fish pokes her head out and wiggles her whiskers, looking as content as can be. "Bizzy's got her purse puppy, and I've got my purse kitty."

"How do you like that?" I bury a kiss in the back of Rudolph's neck. "I guess you're coming with me."

Sherlock barks. *Not me, Bizzy. After lunch I have a serious nap schedule I need to adhere to. I'll see you all for dinner.*

"It's time to get some shopping done," I say, giving Rudolph a quick snuggle.

And hopefully, Eve will help me buy a few clues as well.

Elora's Closet sits at the end of a bustling street in Rose Glen where most of the shops are congregated. The scent of something deep-fried and delicious emits from a fish and chips restaurant across the street, and it's noteworthy to point out there's a bakery a few doors down that has a handful of people pouring into it. I predict I'll be pouring into it soon enough myself. But Elora's Closet has more than a few people pouring into it and it has us taking serious pause before heading in.

"Macy"—I pull her in close by the arm—"don't you think it's weird that there's an equal number of men and women heading inside? I mean, it's a women's boutique. Don't you think that's odd?"

Georgie shakes her head. "I don't know what they're selling, but dibs on whatever it is because I've just all but added it to my inventory."

As soon as Georgie got wind we were heading off to check out Macy's competition, she figured it was her competition, too, and jumped into the back of Macy's car.

Macy grunts, "I knew it was a mistake dragging her out here."

Rudolph belts out a tiny *woof.* **You don't think the killer is in there, do you, Bizzy?**

"You never know," I whisper.

Fish gives a rousing meow. **What's everyone stopping to look at out front?** She nods her nose that way, and sure enough, there's a large framed sign sitting on an easel that people are pausing to examine before they head inside.

"Let's find out," I say.

We migrate over with a robust crowd and something strikes me.

I glance to Georgie and Macy. "Do the two of you notice anything interesting about the people who are flocking their way to the door?"

Macy squints as she examines the masses and gasps.

"Wait a minute." Her mouth falls open. "All these men are hot!"

Georgie makes a face. "And the women look as if they were plucked out of a magazine."

We come upon the sign in question, and while both Macy and Georgie let out a cheer, I groan as if I was just mortally wounded.

"A singles mingle?" I moan at the thought of coming all the way here only to abandon the effort.

"A *holiday* singles mingle," Georgie points out. "But don't worry. The price of admission includes a free Santa hat. That's a bargain, Biz. Those are hard to come by this time of year. Now come on, don't be a grinch. Let's get in there."

"I'm not single, Georgie. And it's *fifty* dollars a person. Serious participants only—it says so right there in the fine print."

"I'm serious, and I'm in." Macy pulls out her compact and checks her face in the mirror. "Plus, I have Fish. Once these beefcakes see my nurturing side, their primal instincts will demand they wife me."

"I'm in, too." Georgie slaps her hands together. "I double dog dare one of these young guns to wife me. There's nothing like the taste of fresh, young, juicy—"

"I get it," I say as Rudolph squirms in my arms.

"Hand him over, Bizzy." Georgie swipes him from me. "I need to demonstrate my nurturing side in the event one of those young guns wants me to pop out a basketball team."

Macy and I opt to take the fifth on this one.

"Okay, fine," Georgie grouses. "This little nugget will be my icebreaker."

"You have never needed an icebreaker," I'm quick to point out. "Me, on the other hand…" I shake my head at the influx of bodies and wonder how in the world I can excavate Eve French from this mingle madness.

Macy links her arm with mine. "You can use your wedding ring as an icebreaker. Come on, I'm buying."

"What? I can't go in there. I'm a married woman."

"Not this afternoon." Georgie links up with my other arm, and soon we're migrating toward the entrance along with the crowd. "Look at it this way. You're vetting these turkeys for Macy and me."

Macy nods. "And I'll make sure you talk to Eve before we leave. Remember, I like them good-looking, funny, and filthy rich. Not necessarily in that order."

Georgie fluffs out her hair. "I'll take 'em in any order I can get 'em so long as they're still breathing. There's always a handful that prefers an intellectual, far more experienced woman." She looks to my sassy sister. "Ten bucks says I'll come away the victor from this denizen of dating."

"Dream on, hippie," Macy says as she antes up at the door, and soon the three of us have all donned red pointy felt hats and are handed a glass of white wine—to ease the pain of that fifty-dollar assault, I'm sure.

It's cozy inside although the store itself looks expansive. A few racks of clothes are scattered about, and beyond that there are a few tables with books and candles strewn over them, but mostly I see people. Soft music bleats over the speakers, but the roar of the crowd and the intermittent laughter are at a far higher decibel.

I'm not a big drinker, but I like the idea of holding something I can splash into someone's face should they get too frisky.

The woman checking us in takes our phone numbers and gives us each a sticker with a code on it to wear over our chests.

She smiles up at us. "Just text back *single and ready to mingle* once you get the alert and then deep dive into the crowd to meet your soulmate. If you see someone you like, just text his code to us, and at the end of the mingle we'll do all the heavy lifting as far as exchanging phone numbers. It's just an extra step in security we like to take. Have a good time!"

My expression sours.

I've already found my soulmate. Another reason I should cut my losses and head to the bakery down the street and stuff my face with cream puffs until this dating disaster is over.

Our phones each ping at once, and we quickly type in the requisite phrase. My phone pings again, and I stare at it a moment.

"That's funny. They just sent me another text."

Macy takes my phone from me and examines it. "Nope, they just sent it once."

"But I could swear I just sent the requisite text back." I back out of the screen and a little yelp escapes me. "Oh no, no, no, no, *no*. I just texted Jasper *single and ready to mingle!*"

A guttural laugh comes from Georgie as she examines my screen from over my shoulder.

"You've got a lot of 'splaining to do, kiddo. Don't worry. Hux is a top-notch divorce attorney. He'll get you out without a hitch to your giddy-up." She presses a kiss to Rudolph's nose, and he pants and looks as if he's smiling from ear to ear. "Turn up the cute stuff, furry pants. We're off to the races." Georgie disappears into the crowd as the music increases a notch—a love ballad Jasper and I danced to at our wedding.

Just great.

I quickly input *single and ready to mingle* once again—into the proper thread and instantly receive a text saying that I'm cleared to roam the premises.

Macy leans in. "Oh geez," she hisses as if she just touched a hot plate. "Dibs on the hulk with the neck tattoo."

"I don't know," I say, craning my neck to get a better look at him. "He looks more like the bouncer you should have at your wedding rather than the groom."

"Who said anything about a wedding?" She pulls Fish out and cradles her like an infant she was about to breast-feed. "I've got my secret weapon. Don't wait up."

"Don't wait up?" I call after her. "But you drove!"

"And just like that, the cheese stands alone," I mutter.

The very married cheese.

My phone bleats in my hand, and it's a text from Jasper.

Is this a role-play thing? Or should I be expecting some legal documents from your attorney this afternoon?

I text right back. **Very funny. Let's go with the first option. Can't wait to see you tonight!** I pepper the text with a bunch of smoochy emojis before I hit *send*, but deep down, I know there aren't enough smoochy emojis in the world to make up for my latest debacle.

A man comes up with wire-rimmed glasses and a greasy smile. Handsome in a shifty sort of way, bald, ruddy cheeks, and pointed nose with a mirror shine. He's swilling his wine my way, and a part of me wonders if that's code for something. I haven't dated in forever. Even before I met Jasper I was pretty rusty in this department.

"Twenty-three." He points to the coded sticker on my chest. "I'm liking what I see. My name is Jack. I work in real estate. You wouldn't believe the master bedrooms I have access to—furnished, too." He waggles his brows. "Cheaper than a hotel. How about it? You ready to play house?"

"Gah!" I turn and quickly shuffle into the crowd. "I do not belong here," I growl out the words in haste as I do my best to spot Eve. Instead, I spot her mini me in the corner with a couple of young girls about her age, and somehow they've managed to snatch Rudolph away from Georgie. It's probably for the better. For some reason, Georgie Conner doesn't need any help in picking up men of any age, and that cute little pup really did put her at an unfair advantage.

"Pardon me?" a deep voice interrupts my thoughts, and I look up to see a tall, handsome steed of a man with a shock of red hair and a toothy smile.

He seems nice in a down-home wholesome way, and for a second I wish I had worn a sticker with Macy's code on it in the event I accidentally bump into her Mr. Right. I could have doubled her inventory for the afternoon.

"Did it hurt when you fell out of Heaven?" he asks. "Because I think you're an angel."

"Yikes." I can't help but make a face.

"That bad, huh?" He winces as if he already knew the answer.

"It's not bad if you were trying to make me laugh. What do you do for a living? I take it you're not on the road honing a comedy routine."

He chuckles, and there's something warm and inviting about him.

"I'm an investment broker. I got corralled into coming here by my brother." He takes a moment to frown into the crowd. "But"—his eyes sweep over my features—"I'm beginning to think this just might be the best thing that's ever happened to me. I'm Brad Wilson." He holds out his hand and gives a sturdy shake. Impressive. Firm, yet not too aggressive.

He leans in and...I think he's sniffing my hair.

I pull back abruptly "I'm Bizzy Baker—*Wilder*." I add that all important last bit quickly. "I just got hitched last September. And would you believe I keep forgetting that I'm married?" A nervous laugh titters from me, but Brad doesn't look so amused.

"What?" His expression irons out. "Did you say you're—married? Geez." He growls out at the crowd, "I knew this was going to be a big waste of time." He stalks off without so much as a goodbye.

"Hey! Wait! I didn't get your number! You'd make a great brother-in-law!" I call out after him, but it's no use.

The sound of a woman tittering from behind sends me spinning on my heels.

Standing before me is a chestnut brunette with deep olive skin, the face of a supermodel, the body of a Victoria's Secret Angel, and the mind and heart of the devil himself. In fact, I'm pretty sure she's a direct relation of that nefarious underworld warlord.

"Camila?" I blurt her name out before I can process what's happening. Camila Ryder is Jasper's ex-fiancée—the same ex-fiancée who happened to weasel her way into becoming his secretary down at the homicide division.

Recently, we've sort of made peace with one another—*sort of* being the operative phrase.

"Don't worry, Bizzy," she says, fiddling with her phone. "I won't say a word to Jasper." Her thumb taps over her screen as she holds up her phone. "They say a picture is worth a thousand words." I see Jasper's name just above a picture of that redheaded man, Brad, sniffing my hair, and I groan at the sight.

"Give me that." I try my best to snatch the phone out of her hand, but it's too late. She's sent him the text.

"Why would you send that to him?" I speed the words out in a panic.

"Why wouldn't I?" She hikes up a notch to get a better look at the crowd. "Five o'clock shadow, red chinos, you're mine." She takes off, and I shake my head at her. Camila deserves whatever Red Chinos has in store for her and then some.

My phone bleats in my hand, and I squeeze my eyes tightly a moment before I have the courage to look at it.

What the hell is happening?

That's what I'd like to know.

"Bizzy?" a woman chimes once again, and I look up, fully expecting to see Camila, but I'm more than pleased I don't.

"Eve!" I practically jump out of my skin with excitement. Thank goodness. I can finally get the inquisition going and make a beeline for that bakery as I try to explain this nightmare away to my husband—that is, if I still have a husband once the day is over. The irony of losing my Mr. Right at an event geared toward finding one isn't lost on me. "Fancy seeing you here." A nervous laugh titters from me. "But I guess you *would* be here. I mean, you own the place."

She offers up a warm laugh of her own. "That would be true. A friend of mine coerced me into hosting the event. Believe it or not, the registers are ringing overtime, so I guess in that respect it's not a bad thing." **And heaven knows I can use the cash.** She shrugs my way. "I just saw your sister, and she mentioned the two of you were coming out to do a little shopping. I guess you got a little more than you bargained for."

I nod. "I'm strictly here for moral support—and to do a little shopping. How are you holding up after the other night?"

Her features darken. "You mean at the inn?" Her eyes shift side to side as if she was about to whisper a secret my way. "I'm not doing well. I was hoping to reconnect with Quinn. I never expected that night to end the way it did." **But I've dreamed of it ending exactly that way for years.**

My eyes spring wide open. "I don't think any of us expected that. How did you know him?"

"Actually, we ran in the same circles. I was just as highbrow as the next billionaire." She makes a face. "Okay, so I didn't quite have billions, but my father left me a comfortable sum."

"That's great. At least you won't have to worry about your financial future." Not that I forgot what Angelica told me. But

I'm fishing to see if their stories line up. Angelica could have gotten the details wrong.

"Nope, the well is dry. I married an idiot and he gambled away my inheritance. After the divorce, I hardly had enough to get this place going. The rent is high, and I barely make ends meet here." **Quinn Bennet was supposed to be my ticket back to Easy Street.** She glowers into the crowd. **And he would have been had he not opened his mouth and shredded me with his words. He knew I couldn't stand to hear those things. But he kept pushing and pushing. Why did he have to push so hard? I couldn't take it. And now I have a broken heart to deal with because he took things too far.**

My lips part as I try to decipher what she meant.

Could she have taken an axe to Quinn? She did say he *pushed* her. I guess even the kindest soul could be moved to murder someone if they're pushed to the edge.

I lift my glass to her. "Here's hoping you have your best sales to date."

She hikes her glass to mine. "And here's hoping they continue on this way forevermore. It's not cheap being a single mother."

"I'm sorry. My mother pretty much raised my siblings and me on her own. My father was still in the picture, and we're on good terms, but she towed the line."

She nods. "Same here." She squints to the back where Elsie and her friends are cooing over Rudolph. "Would you look at that? She's wanted a puppy ever since she was little. Let's hope that cute little thing gives her the puppy fix she needs."

"If she's a true dog lover, this will only make things worse. Rudolph is sort of addictive."

"Hey?" Her brows furrow. "Is that the dog from the other night? The one Santa gave to Quinn?"

"That would be him. I'm taking care of him for now."

"That's so nice of you, Bizzy." She sighs. "Quinn really did like you. We corresponded a few times over the years, and he always brought up the inn. He said the woman who ran it is a saint."

A laugh bucks from me. "Time and distance can put a halo on just about anyone's head."

"Not Quinn's," she quips as she averts her eyes. "He wasn't just a handsome devil. I'm convinced he spent each morning filing down his horns."

"Did the two of you date?" Maybe if I come at it this way she'll offer up a dark confession—at least internally.

She sniffs as she nods. "I thought we would marry, but fate and Quinn had other plans." Her shoulders sag a moment. "You know, I had actually convinced myself that he was the great love of my life. And yet, after seeing him the other night, it became clear I had invented a fantasy version of us that never existed. It was a tough pill to swallow."

Tears gloss her eyes, and my heart breaks for her.

I couldn't imagine being in her shoes—falling in love with Jasper, only to find out he was someone other than I thought.

My phone bleats again, and I don't dare glance at it. There's no way I'm ruining the momentum.

"Eve, what do you think happened to Quinn that night? I mean, outside of the obvious. Who could have done something like that?"

"Oh wow." She blows out a breath. "That's a tough question. Quinn was a pro at infuriating people. You probably weren't familiar with that side of him. It was mostly reserved for friends and family." She glances out at the crowd. "If I had to guess, I'd say this reeks of Arthur."

"Arthur? Arthur Silver?" My eyes widen a notch. Come to think of it, he did do a disappearing act at some point in the night. In fact, he disappeared right after Quinn did.

She nods. "Arthur was his accountant. He did all the heavy lifting as far as paying Quinn's bills, his taxes, his payrolls. Arthur and Quinn were partners in the financial management company Arthur works under. Of course, Quinn promised him the moon—work for me for free and the company is half yours. I don't know all the grisly details, but Arthur has been strapped for cash. He needed a stream of income from his most lucrative client, but Quinn's rationale was that his name brought on the big guns and Quinn could bilk them for all they were worth. It didn't quite work that way I guess. They argued over money. I heard them arguing over it that very night." **Right before I argued with the cold-hearted Brit myself.** Her features harden. "And Arthur is strong. He could have easily swung that axe in a lethal manner. Of course, I couldn't." **With the exception of those rage-fueled moments I had toward the end, but Bizzy doesn't care to know that.** Someone calls her name from afar, and she waves with a laugh. "Would you excuse me? I see an old friend." She darts off, screaming with delight, and I'm left wondering if she made Quinn scream with horror that night.

My phone bleats in my hand again, and I turn it over to see seven more messages, all from a very worried Jasper.

Great.

Let's hope there won't be much screaming tonight once I confess to my husband I spent the afternoon with a room full of single men.

Jasper is levelheaded. I'm sure once I explain it all, he'll understand.

The important thing is that we catch Quinn's killer so we can get on with the holidays.

Next stop on the Homicidal Holidays Express: Arthur Silver.

Christmas is coming, and I have a feeling I'm just a few short steps away from wrapping up a killer and gifting him to the Seaview County Sheriff's Department.

8

The Sugar Plum Tree Lot sits high on a snowy ridge just a short drive from the Country Cottage Inn.

It's dark this evening, but they've got enough string lights up above to make you feel as if you're in a whole new solar system. Throngs of bodies have chosen to congregate here, this snowy December evening. There are bounce houses for the younger set, booths selling hot cocoa and cookies, and even one selling hard hot apple cider and donuts. Santa is here, and oddly he's here in duplicate. Actually, about twelve different men are here dressed as the head elf, and each one seems to be missing that bowl full of jelly belly and housing washboard abs under the red furry suit instead.

"I don't know what that's about," I say, holding Fish close. "And I'm not sure I want to find out."

"Don't worry, Bizzy." Macy pulls back her shoulders with her next breath. "Your big sis is here to protect you from those naughty looking Santas. I'd best go investigate."

"Wait just a minute." Georgie scoops Rudolph from my sister's hands. "The dude magnet stays with me."

"Fine." Macy forces a smile to her face. "I've got a couple of built-in magnets that can make any man howl *ho ho ho*." She takes off, leading with her chest like a woman on a mission to find something sexy in her stocking come Christmas morning.

After that dating debacle at Elora's Closet, I thought it was best I meet up with Jasper on neutral territory, so I convinced him we needed to pick out our tree tonight. And Macy and Georgie opted to hang out as well. And to be honest, despite the chainsaws going off, the never-ending screams of the children, and the potential to have an eight-foot noble topple onto you, this is a far less hostile environment.

A dark laugh strums from Georgie as she cranes her neck past me. "Hang onto your Santa hat, Ruddy. The fireworks are about to go off."

I turn to find Jasper and Sherlock headed this way. Jasper has on a heavy wool coat, and with those broad shoulders of his, it gives him the body of a linebacker. Not to mention those pale silver eyes of his are glowing in the night. His expression is stern, but that only makes him that much more handsome. It's unfair that anger and overall irritation seem to work in his favor. And if I have my way, they'll work in my favor in just a few hours as well.

"Jasper." I give a little hop as I press a kiss to his lips.

Sherlock barks. **_He's not thrilled, Bizzy. But he chuckled a few times on the way over._**

I bite down on a smile. Jasper was probably chuckling to himself because he was plotting on how to get rid of his philandering wife before the new year.

"How was your day?" The words come out a touch too bright. In hindsight, I probably should have emoted a modicum of remorse.

"You go first."

Fish squirms in my arms and mewls, **_You're squeezing the life out of me, Bizzy. Just tell him you were picking up men for the good of the investigation. He'll forgive you._**

Sherlock barks once again. **_If not, there's always bacon. Bacon makes everything better. Can you marry bacon?_**

Sadly, I foresee a frying pan full of bacon in my future, and maybe every day until January as I try to make this up to Jasper. I never thought I'd be bribing my husband to stay in our marriage by way of salted pork fat. And for a second, I marvel at how quickly we devolved to this point.

"Aw, come on, Biz." Georgie elbows me. "Tell him the truth."

Jasper nods. "I'm with Georgie. The truth is my favorite place to start." His expression remains stern but playful. Or not.

"It was Camila's fault." I start right in the middle. "She had no business taking that picture."

Jasper shakes his head. "Wrong answer. Try again."

"Fine. I went to Elora's Closet to help Macy get the lowdown on the competition."

Georgie nods. "And I went, too, for the very same reason. Imagine our surprise when we spotted hundreds of eligible bachelors, all clamoring to get in our pants."

"You're not helping," I'm quick to tell her.

Rudolph gives a few happy *yips* as he struggles to get down. **Tell him about the girls I met and how they're plotting to steal me in the night!**

Good grief.

I bat my lashes up at my ruggedly handsome plus one. "Rudolph just mentioned there are teenagers plotting to kidnap him. We should really beef up security at the cottage."

Jasper shakes his head. "Nice try, but nobody is stealing that dog on my watch."

"That's right." Georgie kisses Rudolph on the top of his head. "They're stealing *you*, Bizzy, right from under Jasper's nose. I saw the way those men were ogling you. There's a bona fide Bizzy Baker Wilder fan club forming right this minute."

"Great." Jasper gives a short-lived smile. "Can I be president?"

"You can be the only member." I swallow down a laugh. "Forgive me?"

"There's nothing to forgive. I hope. Now, what about the case?"

I shrug. "Eve pointed the proverbial candy cane in Arthur Silver's direction."

"And I'll take it from here."

Before I can contest it, Rudolph wiggles his way to the snow and darts under the huge red and white tent where a majority of the trees are set out on display.

"Don't worry, Bizzy!" Georgie takes off. "I'll wrangle him for you."

Sherlock takes off running and barking himself. ***Run, run, Rudolph! There's nothing like slipping and sliding on the fluffy white stuff. You can glide on your paws for a mile, and it makes it feel as if you're flying!***

Fish closes her eyes as she lets out a meow. ***And he'll wonder why his paws are frozen tonight. I suppose I'll have to defrost them once again. A kitten's job is never done.***

Jasper pulls me in and warms me in his arms. "So tell me. How much competition am I up against?"

"Absolutely zero. I only have eyes for you. In fact, I don't even remember the men that were there." I give his bright red tie a quick tug just as my phone bleats and I pull it out. "Ooh, it's Brad Wilson," I say as I bounce on my heels. "He's an investment broker, and I really like him—for *Macy*," I say as I shake my head up at him. "I wasn't *planning* on shopping for a husband for her, but since I had boots on the ground…" I quickly text him Macy's number. "There." I flash my phone at Jasper. "Now they can connect. Just wait until you meet him."

"I cannot wait. I've been meaning to do a little target practice."

A laugh bumps from me as I swat him, and just like that, my phone bleats again.

"Another one?" Jasper is more than mildly alarmed.

"Oh, it's just Jack. He's a raunchy realtor. Him, I don't care for."

"It's nice to know you still have standards."

Fish presses her paws up over my chest. **Who should we gift Jacko to?**

"I'm thinking Jack belongs with Camila." I quickly shoot him her number. "That's what she gets for landing me in hot water to begin with." I wince up at Jasper. "I sort of landed myself there, didn't I?"

"You did." His chest vibrates with a laugh. "I think you're going pro."

Huxley and Mackenzie materialize, and soon Hux has Jasper embroiled in a conversation about a case he's working on. Apparently, Jasper helped arrest the person Hux is defending.

Mackenzie seizes the moment to drag me off to the side by way of yanking my arm. She's donned a long red and white checkered coat, and I loathe how much I'm lusting after it. Her chestnut hair is pulled back and her makeup looks on point. I'm guessing she would have racked up a few more numbers than I did at that slimy shindig earlier. Or if she was in the mood to go old school, she could have just stolen the men who were interested in me like she did back in high school.

Try not to drop me, Bizzy, Fish yowls. ***How dare she touch you like this. I'm suddenly craving a matching set of wicked eyeballs for Christmas,*** she says as she swipes for Mack.

"Hey"—Mackenzie barks down at her—"keep your paws and claws to yourself. If I didn't know better, I'd say you were aiming for my eyes."

An ear-to-ear grin explodes over Fish's furry face. ***It's good to know I can get my point across when needed.***

Mack juts her head my way. "So are you ready to do it?"

"Hold on, girls!" Georgie traipses on over as both Sherlock and Rudolph fly past us and Huxley scoops up Rudolph before he can get away. "Don't get to the juicy parts without me."

"There are no juicy parts," Mack grouses. "This is Bizzy I'm dealing with."

Georgie gives my nemesis a slow wink. "You know her well, I see."

"All right, you two." I take a moment to glare at Mackenzie. "Get to the fun part. I have a handsome husband,

and I want to get to the juicy part of the evening." I shoot a look to Georgie. "Which I am more than capable of."

Mack nods. "That's what I'm here to talk about." She flicks a finger at Georgie. "Scat. I've got something important to discuss, and my time is short."

Fish swipes up at Mack once again. ***Nobody tells Georgie Conner to scat.***

"Fish is right," I say, kissing her on her furry head and not caring one iota that neither human I'm with has any idea of what I'm talking about. "Georgie and I don't have secrets."

"That's right." Georgie postures. "Sure, all of Bizzy's secrets are boring and guaranteed to put even the incurable insomniac to sleep, but it doesn't mean I'll stop pretending to listen to them."

I avert my eyes. "What is it, Mack?"

"You know what it is," she snips. "You're supposed to be helping me set up this proposal."

Georgie gasps. "You're proposing to Huxley!"

"Would you shush?" Mackenzie takes a moment to batter an old woman over the arm. "Keep it down, or the only person who will be surprised will be *you* when you find yourself in traction."

Georgie nods. "I like you, sister. You're spunky."

"She's a walking felony in the making," I say. "Keep your claws off Georgie. Might I remind you there are townspeople here outfitted with cameras? A picture of you beating an old woman is precisely the thing your opponent is looking for."

"*Feh*." Georgie waves it off. "I've known women like this. That's how she initiates people into her bad girls club." She leans. "So tell me, missy. Am I in or am I in?"

Mackenzie sniffs. "You're in."

Georgie whoops and hollers.

"But no funny business," Mack is quick to point out. "Now I need you both to strategize how to best pull this off. Bizzy, what kinds of things does your brother like?"

I make a face. "Mean girls turned mayors with a penchant for terrorizing her constituents. I don't know. You're the one that's looking to marry him. The last thing I remember putting a smile on his face was a mountain of unwashed socks in his room that smelled like vinegar."

Fish mewls, **And now his attraction to Mackenzie Woods makes total sense.**

She's not wrong.

Georgie snaps her fingers. "He likes things that deal with the law. How about you handcuff him to yourself and say meet your new ball and chain?"

"Ixnay," Mack bleats without so much as shedding a smile.

"Bless you," Georgie is quick to tell her. "How about a trip in a hot air balloon? Once you hit the stratosphere, you can pop the question, and if he doesn't say yes, you just tip him over the side. What happens in space stays in space. The world will be none the wiser."

A breath hitches in my throat. "Oh my word, Georgie, didn't you once have a mishap like that with a man in a hot air balloon? Please tell me you didn't push him overboard."

"A girl never kisses and tells."

Fish shudders. *Or shoves and tells either.*

Mackenzie gurgles out a maniacal laugh. "I like you, Georgie Conner. That's more than I can say for you right now, Bizzy. Here she's come up with a half a dozen ideas and you're still stuck on go."

"She came up with two ideas," I'm quick to correct. "And one of them was a felony."

Georgie nods. "I'm sensing a theme here."

I nod because it should be a felony for Mack to propose to anyone, let alone my brother.

Mack leans in. "How did Huxley's other wives propose to him? I'd hate to have a repeat on my hands."

"They didn't." I examine her a moment. "He proposed to them."

She huffs as she looks his way.

Why, I oughta take him home and teach him a lesson. Her mind flits to white noise right after that testy thought. The white noise is more or less a wall of resistance my brain put up once someone's mind decides to take a walk on the raunchy side. And believe me, I'm grateful for the sexy shield. Especially now. The last thing I want is a preview of Mack and the lessons she'd like to teach my brother.

"Fine. I'll think of something," I hear myself say. "He's my brother, after all, and if you've somehow figured out how to cast the right spell to make him happy, then the least I can do is help winnow out the right proposal for him."

Mackenzie sighs as she looks my way. "That was somewhat sweet—despite the fact you threw a zinger into the mix." She checks her phone. "I have to go. The fire department is here shooting a poster for the Cider Cove Christmas Spectacular, and they'll be holding me up as I lie horizontally in their arms." She darts to our right where I see Macy lying horizontally while a herd of shirtless Santas hold her in their arms.

"Hey!" Mackenzie barks. "Get down, Macy Baker! Those are my naughty Santas you're messing with."

Georgie gives a wistful shake of the head. "You're really lucky, Bizzy. She's going to make a great sister-in-law. I always ended up with the fuddy-duddies."

"I'm ending up with something, all right."

"Don't worry, kiddo. You'll always be my favorite fuddy-duddy." She gives me a pat on the back before heading toward the naughty Santa scene herself.

"Hey, wait! I thought I was pretty great."

Hux takes off after his plus one, and Jasper comes my way with both Rudolph and Sherlock running circles around him.

"I think you're pretty great." His brows flex as if he was still as perplexed by my actions as he was when he arrived. "How about finding a tree with me?"

"It's a date," I say.

"Does this mean I made it past round one?"

"Maybe," I tease. "When we get home, I'll let you show me what you've got."

"Challenge accepted. I've got a few night moves I think I can impress you with."

"Ooh, you're confident. I like that." I reach for the nearest tree blindly as I grin up at my handsome hubby. "And I think I like this tree. Our wicked work is done."

"Someone is in a hurry to get home."

"Someone is about to impress me with their night moves. Can you blame me?"

"Not if I'm the one with the moves."

We pay for our evergreen, scoop up our menagerie, and head back to the cottage where Jasper Wilder impresses me with a few new night moves he managed to pull out of his sleeve.

Score one for the singles mingle.

Now to even the score with whoever killed Quinn Bennet.

Arthur Silver had better watch out because I have an axe to grind with him next.

9

The very next day I spend the entire morning and afternoon trying to figure out creative ways that Leo could propose to Emmie, ways that Huxley could propose to Mackenzie, and ways that Mackenzie can propose to Huxley. A part of me proposes my brain take a break from all the proposal madness.

Now if Emmie comes up and tries to enlist me to help her propose to Leo, I'm going to propose we all go out for margaritas and tacos before we hit the Little Chapel of Love on the way home for a couple of quickie nuptials.

Lord knows there isn't enough peppermint bark in the world to help figure this all out. I know this firsthand because I've polished off an entire platter on my own, and now I'm buzzing off a sugar high that there might be no coming down from.

But I needed the distraction of all these potential weddings, and boy, does chocolate ever deliciously distract. And not just from the bevy of brides in my future. Before Jasper left for work, he made me promise on the lives of our furry menagerie that I wouldn't go off on my own to hunt down Arthur Silver. In return, he promised that should he track Arthur down, he'd bring me along on his investigative efforts.

Which is precisely why I find myself in Edison, a seedy town just east of Cider Cove, staring up at this dicey town's famed Radio Hall with a neon flashing sign that reads *The Mistletoettes*, Edison's small town version of the Rockettes. Jasper tracked down Arthur Silver and graciously extended the investigative invite my way.

Mom shakes her head up at the building before us. "I used to bring you and your siblings here every year just before Christmas. That was back when your dad and I were still together and I thought I was taking the family off his hands for a few hours so he could pick up something nice for me for the big day. But as it turned out, he was picking up something nice for himself, the saleswoman at the lingerie shop."

Georgie rocks her head onto Mom's shoulder. "Look at it this way, she was testing out all those lacy frilly numbers for you. I'm sure Nathaniel was only bringing home what he liked."

"Oh, he did," Mom is quick to answer. "He brought home the girl from the lingerie store. She was wife number two."

Juni grunts, "Don't worry, Ree. He did the same thing to me, only it was a girl from the jewelry store. Teaches us to send our husband out for Christmas gifts."

Georgie nudges me. "Where's Jasper?"

I gulp at the thought. "He—uh, fine. He said he needed to pick a special something up for a special someone's Christmas gift, but that he wouldn't miss the show."

Juni ticks her head to the side. "Would that make you or the other woman the special one in this equation?"

Mom growls, "Don't listen to her, Bizzy. Jasper wouldn't dare step out on you."

"Here's hoping," Georgie says as she slings an arm over my shoulders.

This afternoon Jasper called and let me know that he had it on good authority Arthur Silver was coming down to see the Mistletoettes Christmas Extravaganza tonight, and that we should join him—*him* being my ever-faithful husband. And being a longtime fan of the aforementioned show, I wasn't about to say no. I invited my mother to come along, and since Juni and Georgie were at the shop, too, they hopped on board for the leg-kicking express.

We ante up at the front and make our way inside the dimly lit theater with its crimson plush carpeting and walls covered in purple damask. Bodies file in along with us as the crowd rushes to get into their seats. We head over to the coat check and turn in our winter duds, thrilled to expose our holiday attire to one another. I'm still as excited today as I was when I was six over a fancy number to wear on the big day.

Mom and I have each donned a bright red dress—hers being a touch fancier than mine. Georgie has on a red and green tie-dyed kaftan that has already garnered a few stray looks, but Juni is the star, or should I say, spectacle of the show in a short silver number that looks as if it's comprised entirely of tinsel.

"Juni—" Mom gasps, and I'm not sure this is a good thing. Ree Baker has been known to speak her mind a time or twenty, and my father mentioned it was a large variable in his matrimonial disappearing act. "You're like a homing beacon for lost ships." She shields her eyes with her arm and squints for effect. "You'd better sit next to Georgie or I might lose some eyesight tonight. Let's hope no one has a seizure. Did you get that dress off the rack or off a Christmas tree?"

Juni openly frowns at my mother. "You're just loaded with them tonight, ain't 'cha, Ree Ree? I'll have you know, I picked this little number up at Elora's Closet when I drove by this afternoon." She looks to Georgie and me. "Since you two were rude enough not to include me in on the testosterone fun yesterday, I thought I'd run by and see if there were any leftovers I could scoop up. But the next singles mingle isn't until Valentine's Day. Lord knows all my bits and pieces are liable to dry up by then, so I thought I'd seize the moment. When you're my age, every day is Valentine's Day."

Georgie leans in. "The day you sit home alone, binge-watching rom-coms while eating Cherry Garcia straight out of the carton?"

"You betcha." Juni gives a curt nod along with her response.

"You and me both, sister," Mom says "And to be honest? I've liked my Cherry Garcia more than I've cared for most of the men I've dated."

Georgie shakes her head. "Desperate times call for desperate mothers." She snaps her fingers. "I say we set a goal. The three of us are going to have hot dates for Valentine's Day this year. That gives us two months to find a trio of men willing to play the part of Mr. Chocolate Hearts and Billionaire Brains."

Mom rolls her eyes. "You mean Mr. Right Now."

"Let's hold out for the good stuff, Prep." Georgie gives Mom a pat on the arm. "Are chocolate hearts, brains, and billions too much to ask of the universe?"

Mom gives a long blink. "Not if you're living in another solar system. I doubt a man like that exists in ours, let alone three of them."

A man wearing a dark navy suit with a magenta colored tie catches my eyes from across the crowded foyer.

It's him! Arthur Silver.

I recognize that odd hairstyle of his with the shorn look in the back and the moppet up front. He's handsome enough as he laughs while carrying on a conversation with a man who looks suspiciously just like him. Same hair, similar features. The man he's with is currently waving a line of girls in white robes through a door. And each of those women has her hair pulled back into a low bun, copious amounts of makeup on, and I'm pretty sure they're our entertainment for the evening.

"Save a seat for me," I say to my mother before threading my way through the crowd before I lose him.

But I don't lose him. Thankfully, the two men are still locked in an active conversation by the time I arrive and I end up milling around next to them awkwardly. The last of the robed girls dashes through the door, and I step in her place just as the man Arthur is speaking to waves me in close.

His eyes ride up and down my body and he frowns as he glances at my clothes. "Honey, you're late."

My mouth opens as I look to Arthur. "Actually, can I speak with you for a moment?" Arthur has a warmth about him, despite his cheesy smile and that lusty look on his face. His cheeks are covered with dark stubble, and it gives him a bit of a bad boy appeal.

"Not now," the man snips as he ushers me into the room right along with them. "You can talk to my brother after the show. Get to hair and makeup and make it snappy."

"Oh, actually—" I hold up a finger just as a woman dressed in a red T-shirt and green velvet pants yanks me over and gives me a small bag before instructing me to change. I give a quick glance around the well-lit room littered with white robes lying in puddles. Up front there are rows of mirrors lined with clear bright bulbs and seats centered in front of each and every one. Dozens of women are standing around, and each one of them is wearing the same red skimpy dress piped with white feathers—a naughty rendition of a Mrs. Claus costume, I'm guessing.

"Where exactly would I be changing?"

"Right here." The woman in the velvet pants points to the floor, and I give another quick glance around the vicinity.

Arthur and his brother are off to the side, while another girl rushes in and gets dressed right beside me. So I do the only thing I can. I drop trou and do the world's fastest quick change into a red skimpy Mrs. Claus outfit of my own.

An army of women in red and green attack me at once, pulling my hair back, painting my lips. One of them even adheres a Santa hat with a bell to my scalp. And judging by the way she dug those hairpins in, there's no hope of this bad boy ever coming off. I hope Jasper likes the color red because things are going to be festive for quite some time.

A whistle blows, and the girls all fall into single file before trotting out onto stage.

Arthur's brother claps his hands as he does his best to herd the stray girls around the four corners of the room.

"Let's go. Let's go!" he shouts. "Break a leg! All of you."

I cringe just hearing him say it, and watch as he heads off to the side of the stage with them.

A raucous applause breaks out in the distance, and I'm guessing it's showtime.

A woman in red and green comes up clapping my way.

"Get, *get*," she shouts while pointing to the stage.

"I can't go out there." Think—quick! "I don't have shoes."

"Good grief." The stalky brunette looks genuinely panicked. "What size?"

"Seven and a half," I say as she zips off, and I do the same. Only I'm not headed for the stage. I'm headed straight for my number one suspect. The exact man who was missing right after the murder. And I'm going to find out exactly where he went and why. But I think I already know the answer to both of those questions.

I glance down at his hands and huff at the sight of them. I'm betting an axe would fit in them nicely. And speaking of *fit*, he looks as if he can bench-press both Quinn Bennet *and* me. I say he's plenty strong enough to have wielded those fatal blows.

He glances up from his phone and does a double take my way.

"Can I help you?' He offers an affable smile, and a part of me can't help but like him.

Figures. He's one of those charming killers, the kind that's extra nice to you just before he brings down the fatal blow.

"I'm just waiting for my shoes," I say as I inch my way toward him. "Hey, don't I know you?" Asking that question has landed me some of the most noteworthy of suspects in my sleuthing career.

His brows hike a notch. "I'm not sure. But you've probably seen me around. I don't know how many of these shows I've been to, I've lost count. My brother and I are pretty close. I like to support him in all of his endeavors." ***Especially the ones that involve almost nude beautiful women.***

I make a face at him. "That's awfully nice." Somewhat. I couldn't get my sister to come along to see the show, let alone hang out backstage for two hours bored out of her mind while she waited for it to end. Score one for Arthur in the supportive sibling department. "But I think I do recognize you. Weren't you at the Country Cottage Inn the other night? At the Christmas showcase thrown by Quinn Bennet?"

His eyes enlarge for a moment when I say Quinn's name. It was a visceral reaction, that's for sure, but then I supposed just about anyone could have had it.

"Arthur Silver." He holds out his hand, and I shake it.

"Bizzy Baker." I decide to omit my brand new last name in the event it sparks to mind the lead detective that's after him. "I run the inn."

"Ah." His brows hike with amusement. "So you're the manager there. I'm Quinn's accountant. Or I suppose I should say, I *was* his accountant." He winces. "I'm not sure I'll ever get used to that. It's as if it isn't real. Quinn spent most of his time in England, and to be honest, I'm used to not having him around."

A sigh expels from me. "Same here. I feel as if I didn't even get a moment with him that night. Before I knew it, he was gone."

"It's terrible. What a horrific way to go. I hope they catch the beast who did this to him."

"Oh, they will." I lean my ear his way in hopes to pick up on some errant thought floating through his mind, but so far there's zippo. "Say, you wouldn't happen to be a part of the Silver Collective where I send all of my monthly expenses and invoices, would you?"

He belts out a warm laugh. "And don't forget your payroll, too."

"Oh wow"—a genuine smile comes to my face—"and here I thought you were a bunch of robots over there. That's amazing. What a small world. So did you take care of all of Quinn's holdings?"

"Not all. Just the inn and a few smaller properties he needed managed. That's the nice thing about the inn. You were there to manage it for me. Quinn asked me to do it initially, and I did for about three months before I cried uncle. It looks easy enough, but once you get into the day-to-day drudgery, we're talking hard labor. So I gave him the heads-up and he hired someone right out the gate—eye candy he called her. He said she'd be good to drive in traffic with the twenty to sixty age demographic."

"That's quite a spread," I say, completely unamused.

He waves it off. "That was about six years ago. When did you start up there?"

"About six years ago."

We share another warm laugh, and I'm actually enjoying being in his company. If he asked me to hand him a nearby axe, I'd probably do it.

I lean in a notch. "So did you get a chance to speak with him that night?" I'll admit, it feels as if Arthur has suddenly morphed into an old friend. In a way he's more than an acquaintance—we shared the same boss.

Arthur closes his eyes a moment too long. "I sure did speak with him that night." ***And I let him have it, too. I shouldn't have gone. I certainly shouldn't have gotten so worked up over petty grievances. Not that withholding cash from me was petty. How did the guy expect me to live?***

That sounds in line with what Eve was telling me.

"So was Quinn one of your largest clients at the Silver Collective?"

His expression sobers up and his chest thumps with a silent laugh.

"He was my partner in the management company. Let's just say he was the silent partner." ***Who collected all the coins I managed to scrape up, while I was left with goose egg.***

"So how does that work? Quinn didn't have a say in any of the business dealings?"

A laugh cracks from him. "No, that wouldn't have been Quinn if he did. He put up the capital to get the company going. I came in as a squirrely kid. I met Quinn when he was making the casinos rich back in the day. I worked the blackjack table and we grew to be friends." **Or so I thought.** "I always wondered what he saw in me to trust me enough to be the accountant with his personal and business finances." **And now I know it was my naïveté he was looking for.** "I was fresh out of college with a dual degree in business and accounting. Anyway, here I am."

"So what happens now? I mean, I guess you get the whole company, right?"

He tips his head to the side. "I don't know. But I'm not counting my chickens before they're hatched. Quinn always had an ace up his sleeve." **And it always worked as a loss for me. I can't believe I went years living off skimpy bonuses. Here I am an accountant without a steady income of my own, still living in my brother's basement.**

I take a quick breath, sorry for the poor guy.

"The reading of the will is coming up this Monday at two. It'll be at the inn."

"I've been invited by his attorney. I guess I'll find out all the grisly details that day with everyone else. I suppose you'll be there, too."

"Oh, I will. In fact, I'll have refreshments on hand." I press my lips tightly a moment. "Arthur, did you happen to see Quinn, you know when he was—"

I let my words hang in the air and he shakes his head.

"No, thank goodness. After the show wrapped up, I had a few words with him." Same irate words I had with him before the show. His mind goes gray, and I inch back because I've never experienced that before. "Let's just say things weren't friendly between Quinn and me that night. I guess I should say I'd take it all back, but that conversation was long overdue." ***Thank goodness for the hot blonde who caught me on the way out and told me she could make all of my troubles disappear—did she ever. Lucky for me, she said she worked there and happened to have the key to an empty room, and boy, did we ever take advantage of it.***

My mouth falls open. How in the heck did this woman get a key? I'm going to have to fire Grady, Nessa, and myself for ineptness. I don't care if a murder did take place at the inn. That's no excuse for someone having access to the holy grail.

Wait a minute...

I clear my throat. "Well, too bad we didn't meet that night. My sister works the inn sometimes." Or at least she pretends to. "Her name is Macy? A touch taller than me, short blonde hair, ice blue eyes, very sassy."

He cocks his head. "Doesn't ring a bell." But sounds just like the woman I was with, Tracy, to a T."

I make a face just as the woman dressed in red and green comes at me with a pair of size seven and a half tap shoes with heels.

"Get these on and get out there, stat! It's almost time for your big moment. You've got the hat with the bell that means you're the pinwheel, remember?" She drops to her knees and helps latch my feet into the shoes.

"Arthur"—I pant as my body is jostled—"who do you think could have done this to Quinn?"

He ticks his head back a notch as he scans the ceiling.

"You know, no one was closer to him than Warwick. Quinn trusted that man like a brother."

"I think he trusted you like a brother, too. You were in charge of all the finances."

Arthur chuckles at the thought. "Not quite. He had more checks and balances in our company, you'd think he had hired a den of thieves to run it." *And I would have been one if I thought I could have gotten away with it.* His expression sours. *After that last stunt he pulled, I should have swiped the money anyway. He's dead now. That's all that matters. The man can't torment me a day longer. And I've never breathed easier.*

"So Warwick was his trusted friend?" I bet Warwick will know exactly what was truly going on between Quinn and Arthur.

"Yup. Warwick and Quinn had some business dealings, too, but that's all kept separate from the Collective, so I don't know too much about it. Telecommunications stuff. That's where Quinn's real payday was coming from. No offense, but that little inn wasn't keeping him in his jet setting lifestyle."

"No offense taken."

The girl working on my shoes slaps me on the thigh.

"Now get! *Get!*"

Arthur laughs. "I'll see you at the reading of the will, Bizzy. Nice meeting you!"

I'm quickly shuffled onto stage and overcome with a flash of white-hot lights pouring down over me while "Santa Claus is Coming to Town" blares throughout the cavernous room.

A girl with a white version of the accouterment the rest of us have on links arms with mine and quickly lands me in the middle of the melee as the girls line up to my right and left, with one row facing one way and the other facing in the opposite direction.

The girls to the right and left of me link arms with mine, and soon we're moving in a slow and steady circle to the delight of the crowd.

The crowd! Oh my word. Is it awful to hope that Jasper got a flat on the way? Perhaps a small fender bender that requires an auto shop?

A couple of girls scoop me up from behind, and before I know it, I'm in the air, moving toward the front of the stage, ten feet off the ground at least.

"Hands up!" the girl to my left shouts, and instinctively I raise my arms into the sky. And just as the song comes to a close, an explosion of red and green pyrotechnics explodes from either side of the stage.

The audience is on their feet, and I hear Georgie and Juni screaming my name with glee.

The song ends, the women remove their arms, and I fall softly into another set of Mistletoettes' arms.

We walk off stage in single file, and I jump back into my clothes, much to the screaming chagrin of the red and green brigade.

"Keep the shoes," I shout as I kick them off and land in the flats I came in. I rush right out of the side door, only to find throngs of humanity pouring into the foyer as the intermission begins.

I spot my mother, Georgie, and Juni at the front of the concession stand clamoring for popcorn and T-shirts. Here's hoping they get me an extra-large in both the popcorn and the T-shirt. Souvenir shirts from the theater are my favorite to sleep in.

"Excuse me, miss?" an all too familiar voice strums from behind, and I freeze solid before spinning on my heels to see the most gorgeous man I've ever seen in my life holding out a red bouquet of roses. Jasper dips his chin as he shoots me a look. "Can I have your autograph?"

"I'm sorry, sir. I only give them out naked and in bed. But I'm pretty sure I have a vacancy for the evening. My husband has had it with me." I bite down over a smile as he hands me the flowers and I bury my face in them.

His chest rumbles with a dark laugh as he pulls me in. "I'll take that spot. Your husband sounds like a donkey." He winces. "Bizzy, you scared me to death. I almost rushed to the stage to catch you. You could have broken a leg."

"That sounds like something my husband would say." I pull him in close by the tie. "Because he loves me. How about we stock up on nachos and M&M's before the lights flicker?"

"All right, but I'm taking you to dinner afterwards. It's the least I can do before I get that autograph."

"Sounds like a delicious plan."

"That and I think we're going to need to fuel up for the big endeavor."

We meet up with my mother, Georgie, and Juni who come bearing T-shirts and popcorn for me included. We sit and enjoy the rest of the Mistletoettes pre-performance, and when the show is over, Jasper and I pick up some takeout and make a beeline for the cottage. I tell Jasper everything I gleaned from Arthur Silver, and when I'm done, we make a pact not to speak of the case for the rest of the night. We have far more interesting topics to explore.

And when all is said and done, I put on a whole other performance, a private show just for Jasper.

Arthur Silver is still on the suspect list. He has a motive. He said himself that he spoke to Quinn after the show, which could put him right at ground zero when that axe went swinging. Now to corroborate his story about a certain blonde named *Tracy*.

Who knows? She might just hold the missing link to this entire case.

Macy Baker, hold onto your sassy skirt because I'm coming for you next.

10

Main Street in December in and of itself is magical, but add snow to the equation and it's as if we've left reality and landed in a fairytale.

It's almost one in the afternoon and things have fallen just a touch behind for the official grand opening of my mother and Georgie's new shop. There were delivery issues, shelves that kept falling apart, and the last-minute software glitch on the ultra-modern register system. But it seems as if it's finally all systems go as an entire mob has gathered outside to help usher in this victorious moment.

The crowd is thick with mostly women, and mostly women of a certain age, each one rubbing their proverbial hands together looking as if they can't wait to rush inside and part with their money. Honestly, they're most likely rubbing their hands together so they won't fall off. And I'm guessing the reason they want to rush inside has to do with getting out of the elements. But still, the sentiment is nice.

A refreshment table has been set out front with coffee, hot cocoa, cider, donuts, and mounds of peppermint bark—all provided by the Country Cottage Café, of course. The doors to the establishment have been painted bright red, and there are curtains hung over the windows in an effort to build the suspense of what these shiny new patrons might find inside.

Up above the entry a sheet is draped over the wooden sign, leaving the people to wonder what the name of this shop might be as well. It's not a marketing concept I would have gone with for opening day, but nonetheless they have plenty of prospective customers here ready to storm the castle, so it seems to be working.

"Mom"—I laugh while bouncing Rudolph in my arms—"where did all these people come from?"

She gives me a look. "You know, Georgie. I told her to spread the news, and she shot it across the four corners of Cider Cove like a cannon filled with rainbow glitter. She's got every senior center, senior club, and any organization that had anything to do with Christmas out here today. Let's hope they like what they see inside." *And that they brought lots of cold, hard cash to throw at the register.*

Georgie and Juni step our way, right along with Mackenzie Woods. Georgie has Fish tucked on the inside of her coat, and I can see one of her wonky quilt dresses peeking from underneath.

Juni, too, is wearing a wonky quilt dress along with a wonky jacket thrown over that. It looks as if she's doubling down her wonky sense of fashion in a show of solidarity for her mother.

Mayor Mackenzie Woods, however, is clad in somber black from head to toe, and has chosen to accessorize the cheery look with a sourpuss on her face. I still find it hard to believe she and Hux are determined to get hitched to one another.

Mackenzie nods to my mother. "I'll say a few words first. And Hux has a bottle of champagne, if you want to smash it over something and christen the place once the sign is revealed." *Bizzy's head would be my pick.*

I avert my eyes at that one.

Mom scoffs. "And have a mess of broken glass all over the sidewalk? *Please*, I could just see the lawsuits now. No thank you. I'll take that bottle home. Something tells me I'm going to need it."

Juni moans at the thought. "I'll split it with you, sister. I've got a full-time job here, too, you know."

"Yeah," Mom says. "And coincidentally as our one official employee, you're the only one pulling a paycheck at this point."

Mackenzie shrugs. "No champagne. Have it your way. We can throw a donut at the wall and christen it for all I care." She stalks off to the front where Hux is speaking to a few of the customers in line, and they all seem to be laughing and having a good time.

"All right, Toots." Georgie elbows my mother before pointing up at the sign. "Whatever Macy decided is what it's going to be. Full disclosure, I've been picking up her lunch for the past two weeks."

"Full disclosure"—Mom huffs a laugh—"I gave birth to her almost thirty years ago. You'll just have to read it and weep."

"What's Macy deciding?" I ask with a note of caution. Macy has made many decisions in her life, most of them dicey.

Georgie gives a dark chuckle. "The fate of the world, kiddo. The fate of the world."

Fish mewls, **Anyone with half a brain knows you don't leave decisions of any magnitude in Macy's hands. These two must have been very desperate. But Macy does have a way of being brutally honest. In fact, that day Macy found me behind her shop, she looked right at me and said, 'I'm not keeping you no matter how cute you look. Let's see if my sister is a sucker.' I'm so glad you were a sucker, Bizzy.**

"Me too," I whisper as I wrinkle my nose her way. She knows it's my favorite story. And true as gospel, I've never been happier to be a sucker.

Rudolph lets out a yip of a bark as he wiggles in my arms. **Macy says my puppy dog eyes can make her do things that aren't rational—like try to adopt me.**

I shake my head him. "And I would never let that happen."

Mom grunts, "Bizzy is right. We should have never let Macy have the final say in what we should call the store." She frowns my way. "We would have asked you, but we needed someone ruthless. We narrowed it down to two options, but we couldn't decide. Of course, I said we should flip a coin."

Juni raises her hand. "I flipped it myself."

Georgie smacks her lips. "That coin was rigged, and you both know it."

Mom tosses up her hands. "I won three out of three—fair and square."

"What were the choices?" I cock an ear their way. "I could be ruthless. I'll tell you right now what I would have chosen and we can see if Macy and I are truly like-minded."

Georgie twitches her brows at my mother before looking to me. "Ree and Georgie—or Georgie and Ree. Now which one would you have picked?"

Juni balks, "My vote was for Juniper Moonbeam's Delights. Who wouldn't want to go in there and drop every dollar they own?"

Mom chuckles. "Anyone not on psychedelic drugs, that's who."

"Already being mistreated by the management." Juni shoots her a look. "The only thing to keep me from quitting is a steady stream of donuts." She takes off for the refreshment table, and I'm half-tempted to join her.

Rudolph barks. ***Don't pick, Bizzy. Sherlock says Christmas is coming and we need to be on our best behavior if we want to find bacon in our stockings.***

"I plead the fifth," I tell them. "I'd like to find bacon in my stocking." I glance to my right and spot Jasper coming this way along with my father and his mother.

"Bizzy Bizzy!" Dad envelops me in a warm hug before I can smile his way. Nathan Baker has jet-black hair, light eyes, and a smile that never leaves his face. My father has always greeted me that way, doubling up my name and singing it out loud. That's my father in a nutshell, the forever jovial boy who never grew up. Sure, he's had a string of failed marriages, but I think he rather appreciated the short-lived nature of those matrimonial stints. He worked as a finance manager before retiring. And just last year he tried to recruit Jasper's mother, Gwyneth, as his next wife, but she wisely opted to have a long engagement instead. Shockingly, they're still together.

Gwyneth is tall, thin, tight-lipped, has a halo of black hair, and the same pale eyes as Jasper. I'm not her favorite person, but she seems to tolerate me well enough. And honestly? The feeling is mutual.

We exchange niceties, and soon my mother and Gwyneth are embroiled in a conversation about how chaotic the holidays can be. Kudos to my mother for actually forging a friendship with almost all of Dad's wives and girlfriends. If that were me, I'd shoot them on sight. Okay, so that's a little harsh. But I'd shun them on sight, for sure.

And speaking of sights, the best one yet is headed this way. Within a minute Jasper wraps his arms around me as Sherlock barks and jumps by his side.

I knew he'd show up, Bizzy. I knew he would. I just finished marking the doors. This store is as good as mine.

Georgie takes Sherlock's leash and quickly parades him around with pride.

"Glad I didn't miss it." Jasper lands a heated kiss to my lips that warms me down to my bones. He pulls back with a loose grin on his face. Let's just say the things that happened behind locked doors last night were enough to leave a silly grin on both of our faces for the next ten years. Who knew Jasper has always had a hankering for the Mistletoettes?

"You didn't miss a thing," I say, dusting the snow off his shoulders. "I just found out Macy was the deciding factor on what they named this place." I quickly relay the choices and he laughs. "That's actually tougher than it seems."

Emmie hops this way with a platter of her peppermint bark, and both Jasper and I indulge.

"Jasper"—Emmie glances over her shoulder—"Leo was just looking for you. It sounded important."

"I see him there across the street." Jasper gives him a wave. "I'll be right back."

He takes off, and Georgie comes over with Sherlock and Fish.

Sherlock barks up at Rudolph and does his best to nip the puppy's tail. ***Get down here in the white stuff! It's cold, makes you run twice as fast, and you can eat it, too!***

Fish yowls and swipes her paw in Rudolph's direction. ***Don't eat the yellow snow!***

Emmie laughs. "I don't need to be a mind reader to know he wants down."

"You would be right," I say, doing just that and lengthening his leash in the process. "Sherlock wants to share his love of the frozen white stuff."

Georgie rubs her hands together and looks my way. "Speaking of white stuff, how's the proposal planning coming?"

Emmie takes in a sharp breath. "Oh my goodness! Is Leo going to propose?" Her eyes bug out at the thought, and she's clutching onto my arm with a death grip.

"Sorry, Toots." Georgie is quick to shoot Emmie off the proverbial altar. "But Hux is set to propose to Mayor Woods," she whispers that last part, and thankfully so, seeing that they're standing ten feet away. "Get *this*—Mack is going to propose to Hux. And the kicker is—they've both enlisted Bizzy to help get the job done."

Emmie groans as she looks my way. "Talk about being forced to drink a cup of vinegar. I can't believe you didn't tell me this. It's kind of hysterical. I mean, we both love Hux and we want the best for him. But Mack?" She glances skyward. "I guess we'll have to live with what fate has given us, at least for as long as they can hold their breath as one. I give it a year."

"I'm with you on that." I nod. "Although, my worst nightmares have been known to come true, and having Mack strapped to my family like a bomb for the next fifty years might just be one of them."

Georgie clucks her tongue. "You never know. She could end up finding her way into the inner sanctum again. Weren't the three of you besties once upon a time? It could happen again." She takes Rudolph's leash from me and takes off with a couple of happy puppies.

Emmie makes a face. "Did she just put a hex on us?"

"The very worst kind."

Mackenzie gets the show on the road by way of ringing a bell, obnoxiously loud and quick.

"Hear ye, hear ye!" Mackenzie bellows the words out in a bullhorn. "As the Mayor of Cider Cove, I'd like to welcome another female-owned business to the family of respectable establishments right here on Main Street. Without further ado, let's reveal the name of this place so we can get inside and knock out the rest of the names on our shopping lists!"

A cheer breaks out as Hux climbs a ladder and gives the sheet that covers the sign a hard yank.

It takes a moment for the crowd to let the name of the shop sink in before a raucous laugh breaks out all up and down Main Street.

"*Two Old Broads?*" Mom barks it out like a threat as she looks past me.

Emmie and I turn to find Macy wrapped in a forest green coat while giggling herself into a conniption.

"My work here is done." She beams a smile of satisfaction as the doors to the new establishment are opened and the crowd drains inside.

Mom gags and chokes her way over. "Macy Ree Baker! How dare you humiliate me like this!"

Hux comes over with a laugh caught in his throat. "You did good, sis."

"Two Old Broads!" Georgie shouts with glee as she runs from inside the shop. "I knew you wouldn't let me down, Macy Baker! Now get in there and show 'em how it's done."

Macy gives a long blink. "You mean shopping?"

"No, the register is malfunctioning again. I keep yelling at it, and it's still keeping its moneymaking mouth shut."

Macy gives a hard groan. "I told you this is not a voice command unit—they don't exist. You need to input your password each time you want to use it. I've got a solution. Why don't we just send all these nice folks to my shop instead?"

I take the leashes from Georgie as my sister pulls her into the store with marked exasperation.

Mom shakes her head. "I'd better get in there before Georgie decides to give everything away for free so she doesn't haven't to deal with technology."

Georgie pokes her head out the door. "Everything is free for the next few hours! Tell a friend!"

"She's kidding!" Mom shouts so loud her voice nearly breaks the sound barrier. "Nothing is free! Nothing is ever free, *Georgie*."

Hux grunts, "They're going to kill each other, and then we'll have to change the sign to read two *dead* old broads."

"Speaking of killing." Emmie leans his way. "Bizzy just told me the news. Hope you don't mind. So you're really popping the question? Have you narrowed down the proposal possibilities? I mean, this is huge, Hux. You can't mess this up."

His cheek cinches as he looks my way. "That's why I've got Bizzy on it." He squints over at Emmie. "If Leo were to propose, how would you want it done?" ***I'm shocked Bizzy hasn't already gone this route with her.***

I'm shocked, too.

Emmie takes a breath. "Oh, I'd want it done on a night that has meaning, you know, a birthday, an anniversary, a holiday, Christmas!" She snaps her fingers. "Christmas Eve would be perfect. I'd want it semi-private but with lots of family nearby, so that when I said yes we could all celebrate together." She taps her chin as she considers this. "I always thought it'd be cute if he staged a fight. You know, if he gave me the impression he was going to break up with me, and then when I panicked he dropped to one knee."

"Stage a fight..." Hux glances to the side, and you can practically see his wheels churning. His phone buzzes, and he gives it a quick once-over. "Duty calls. Glad I could be a part of this mess." He kisses me on the cheek. "We'll talk about the big day. I'll see you girls later. And remember, it's a secret."

"My lips are sealed!" Emmie pretends to zip her mouth shut as he takes off, and a part of me wishes she had done just that a moment ago.

"Are you insane, telling him to pick a fight with Mack? Have you met her? Arguments of any kind are the very thing that nourishes her wicked soul. She'll chew my brother a new one before he ever gets on one knee. In fact, if he falls to the floor, she might just drive her stiletto through his heart."

Emmie bucks with a laugh. "You're so right. I'm sure whatever you have planned is way better."

I wince. "Any other ideas? You know, something *you* might actually like?"

"I don't know." Her gaze drifts across the street where Jasper and Leo are steeped in a conversation. "If Leo were to propose, I don't think I'd want him to pick a fight with me. I'd want him to do something sweet, like bury my ring in a slice of chocolate cake. That way we can start our journey as a family in the sweetest way possible." She cranes her neck toward the refreshment table. "Speaking of sweets, I'd better restock the donuts and the peppermint bark."

I snatch another piece of bark from the platter in her hands as she leaves, and Macy snatches one off it as she comes my way.

"My evil work is done," she says, snapping off a bite with her teeth.

"Which evil work? Giving a rather appropriate name to Mom and Georgie's shop? Or the fact you pretended to be an employee of the inn the night of the murder and lured a man by the name of Arthur Silver to a private suite so you could have your way with him?"

Her brows hike. "Was *that* his name?"

"Would you knock it off?" I swat her. "Yes, that was his name. How long have you been imitating an innkeeper just to satiate your *insatiable* appetite?"

"Please." She darts a glance to Heaven. "When you're lucky enough to have a sister that practically owns an inn, you don't look a gift horse or a free room in the mouth."

"I've never given you a free room."

"Not intentionally. And thank you, by the way."

"Don't thank me. You're lucky I don't have you arrested."

Jasper comes up just as I say the words.

"Are we arresting Macy?" He looks almost amused by the thought.

She glares over at him. "You *would* take her side."

He shrugs. "I'm sleeping with her. What's the offense?"

I look up at him. "She was sleeping with Arthur Silver the night Quinn died. You're looking at the exact reason he wasn't in the ballroom after the murder."

Macy gasps and clutches at her throat. "Please tell me I didn't sleep with the killer."

"I had Leo look into the guy." Jasper rocks back on his heels. His expression darkens a notch. "Let's just say if he did kill Quinn, it wouldn't be his first foray into murder."

My mouth falls open. "You mean he's killed before?"

Jasper nods. "And he just might have done it again."

11

As fate, good luck, or dumb luck would have it, the women of Cider Cove can't get enough of a quaint new little shop called Two Old Broads. It turns out, not a customer walks into their shop that doesn't bring up the colorful moniker.

Who knew a feisty name would be all they needed to get hordes of people to part with their hard-earned dollars?

My feisty sister, that's who.

The next day I spend all of my free time trying to nail down Warwick Tully. According to Arthur, no one was closer to Quinn than Warwick. And ironically, I'm hoping he'll be able to shed some more light on Arthur Silver.

Yesterday, Leo shared with us that Arthur was charged with killing a man on a hunting trip during his senior year in high school. On the outset it looked as if it should have been accidental, seeing that Arthur shot the man from a decent distance, but witnesses say they saw Arthur arguing with the man earlier that morning. It was a friend of his father's, who was later discovered to have been having an affair with Arthur's mother.

The court ruled it as criminal negligence, and Arthur was held in a juvenile detention center during the proceedings and released for time served once the verdict was given. Arthur claimed he was aiming for a buck and never saw the man who took the bullet. Lucky for Arthur, there was another hunter with him who not only claimed to see the buck, but corroborated Arthur's claim that the man he shot came out of nowhere. The hunter corroborating Arthur's story was his brother. A part of me wonders if the brother wanted the cad that was seeing his mother dead just as much as Arthur did.

And tonight I'm hoping to gain a little more clarity on the type of person Arthur is, and more importantly, if Quinn ever said anything about him to Warwick.

"Hubba hubba." Georgie moans as she inspects a couple of frat boys walking into Quinn's Bar and Bistro, out in Whaler's Warf, and that's exactly where we stand now.

I had no idea Quinn owned a bar out in Whaler's Warf. I vaguely remember him telling me about other establishments he held in Maine, but once he assured me they weren't inns, I guess I must have tuned him out.

Regardless, it turns out, this place is a nightly haunt for the next suspect on my list. And per the contract I seemingly entered into with the lead homicide detective on the case, I informed him of my whereabouts and he said as soon as he was done with forensics he'd swing on by. Besides, I'm far from alone. I have Macy, Georgie, and Juni with me.

"Georgie, stop drooling," Macy snips as she adjusts her booty-hugging little black dress.

She's chosen to spice up the much-loved frock with a pair of spiked silver heels.

Believe me, I've got my eye on those, and if she pulls any unwarranted stunts, I might accept them as payment for letting her tag along on my little investigative jaunt. I caved this time once she swore she'd never sleep with a killer again.

Macy sniffs my way. "Those boys were young enough to be embryos. I should have figured that when you invited me out for a bar crawl something would be amiss. I don't do frat boys. Here's hoping a scruffy bartender who doubles as a vampire can rectify the night." She cinches her purse over her shoulder as she marches on in.

"Don't forget the booze!" Juni shouts after her. "Booze always rectifies the night for me."

I hold the door open for the rest of our motley crew, only to find Macy in the foyer donning what looks to be reindeer antlers with tiny bells festooning them and a red plastic nose that blinks on and off.

"You're going to pay for this," she hisses while wagging a finger my way. "You're lucky they serve beer." She stalks on into the heart of the establishment just as the hostess welcomes us and hands us each a set of antlers and a glowing red nose for ourselves.

"Fair warning"—the hostess shrugs—"the Greeks from Dexter University are hosting their Christmas bash here tonight. It might be a little rowdier than usual."

"Really? I went to Dexter." It comes out a little too enthusiastic. I didn't graduate, but I doubt anyone is going to ask me to pull out my college records tonight.

The hostess laughs. "Then you know exactly how rowdy they can be."

I quickly scan the establishment, with its dusty wooden floors, small round tables, packed dance floor, and what looks to be a thousand lunatics running around disguised as Santa's most trustworthy reindeer. Everyone is either laughing hysterically or gyrating their limbs as if they were being electrocuted.

"Honestly, the three of us might just be the sanest people in the room tonight." I purposely left Macy out of the equation because her sanity has been questionable from an early age. I turn to look at Georgie and Juni and freeze.

Georgie has attached herself onto Juni's back and is spurring her onward with her invisible reins.

"Never mind," I say. Honestly, with Juni's barely-there leather getup and Georgie's neon green kaftan, it only adds to the visual. "Let's get seated and see what's on the menu."

"Oh"—the hostess holds up a finger—"we're sort of famous for our bacon wrapped jalapeño poppers."

Juni makes an odd wailing sound as she stalks forward. "Jalapeño poppers and boozy boys? Something tells me this is going to be a night to remember."

I'm about to ask the hostess where I can find Warwick when I spot the stalky man himself at the bar, patting a patron on the back as they share a laugh together.

Georgie and I follow Juni inside as a country version of a holiday song croons overhead. Macy is nowhere to be seen. For all I know, someone could have hauled her off to the alley and buried an axe in her. And seeing that she has a propensity to sleep with my prime suspects, this could be a very real possibility.

We find a table near the bar, and it affords me a straight shot of the suspect at hand. Warwick has donned the requisite antlers and impossible to breathe through red rubber nose. He's wearing a suit that stretches to accommodate his barrel chest, and a few of the buttons on his dress shirt look as if they're being compromised.

A waitress blocks my view momentarily, and Juni puts in four orders of bacon wrapped jalapeño poppers.

"Four?" I balk as the waitress does a disappearing act.

"You don't know what Mama and I are capable of when it comes to spicy food." Juni nods, and the bells attached to her antlers give a little jingle.

"Georgie, I thought you had a sensitive stomach?"

"Not when it comes to anything wrapped in bacon. How hot can it be? And don't worry, Biz. If we have any leftovers,

I'll take some back to my cottage. I've got a backlog of mixed martial arts on my DVR just waiting for me to pair it with a spicy snack."

"Good idea," Juni says. "I'll take a few back to Sprinkles."

"You can't feed that to Sprinkles," I spit the words out in a flurry. "That's like sticking a firecracker into a five pound piñata."

"Oh, honey"—Juni looks sick at the thought—"she's not shooting candy out of her rear. I've been finding those Tootsie Rolls of hers all over the house." She says *Tootsie Rolls* with air quotes.

"That's too bad," I say. "Maybe you should take her out to go potty a little bit more?"

Her face smooths out. "You mean I'm supposed to take her out?"

The waitress comes back with four huge orders of poppers and a round of ice water.

"Something stronger, sister," Juni insists as she pushes the water aside. "Give me the house special."

"And I'll take what she's having," Georgie says.

The blonde in a tight little blue dress nods. "Two tequila slammers coming right up. And you, miss?" She offers to put one in for me and I quickly decline.

The three of us dive right into those bacon-covered delights—some of us with far more vigor than others—and soon both Georgie and Juni are pounding their fists to the table and stomping their heels to the floor. Interestingly enough, their silent cries for help happen to coincide with the rhythm of the music, and soon the entire establishment seems to be joining in on the foot stomping fun.

Both Georgie and Juni shove glasses to their faces, and water and ice alike go flying.

"Elegant." I wink over at them as they pant and gasp.

"Danger danger, Will Robinson!" Georgie shouts.

"I doubt anyone in here is old enough to remember that." I shrug. "But I do and I can appreciate the warning."

"Don't worry, Mama." Juni gives a few hard blinks as the tears start flowing and her mascara melts into a muddy river. "I'll box 'em up. This will feed the dog for a month."

"What?" A choking sound emits from me. "What part of that firecracker in the piñata euphemism didn't you understand?"

"Never mind that." Georgie swills her water my way. "We've got a proposal to plot."

"Oh, is it Emmie's?" Juni bounces in her seat as if she were the one Leo was about to propose to.

Georgie waves the idea off. "Emmie's got this in the bag. I say we plot Hux and Mayor Woods' budding fiasco. And get this—they're both proposing to *each other*."

I nod. "And they've both asked me to plan out the mockery to matrimony. Juni, you've been married a few times. How did all your future exes pop the question?"

"Let's see"—she squints at the ceiling—"Junior flashed his knife my way and, of course, I said hell yeah. I just had my nails done and didn't want to deal with having blood on my hands."

"His or yours," I muse.

"Both." Her head ticks to the side. "Then there was your daddy. I darn near fell out of bed when he asked."

"I did not need to know that." Speaking of blood relatives, I glance around to make sure Macy is still alive and spot her doing a spicy version of the two-step out on the dance floor. "And number three?"

Juni shrugs. "It was some guy I met at a bar in Edison. We were riding the mechanical bull together and he said, 'If you don't fall off, I'm marrying you.' It was a threat he made good on."

"Smooth," I say as the rhythmic clapping from the dance floor hits new heights.

A loud whoop followed by chanting comes from the right and we see a girl doing a handstand on what looks to be a keg of beer. About three beefy men are holding her in the position while a young brunette who looks all of thirteen shoots beer into her mouth. The woman's blonde hair dangles around her face, and I can't help but notice she's wearing a pair of silver spiked heels.

"Hey, those shoes look familiar," I say, standing up, and sure enough, my saucy big sis is having liquor streamed right into her pie hole.

"Wait a minute." Juni jumps to her feet as well. "Nobody outperforms me when it comes to keg stands." She takes off like a leather-clad bullet as Georgie stretches by my side.

"Welp. I'm ready," she announces.

"To leave?" Because so am I.

"Are you kidding? We're not leaving until we've cuffed the perp and roughed him up with a butter knife."

My lips twist. "I don't think we'll be assaulting anyone with a butter knife tonight. Besides, I actually like tonight's mark. I think he has some information that might help me nail the killer. In fact, that's my mark right over there." I nod to the bar where Warwick sits ensconced with a blonde on either side of him.

"Well hello, hot and hairy. I'm calling dibs on this one, Biz. I specialize in furry men with a little extra to hold onto at night." She makes a beeline his way, and I quickly follow.

Note to self: Clearly delineate to all parties I may have inadvertently hauled along with me, that under no condition are they allowed to hit on suspects. It's bad enough Macy might have had her way with the killer, right after he had his way with Quinn by way of an axe.

And I need Warwick willing to talk about suspects, not planning a covert op at Georgie's cottage that may or may not involve nudity. And for the love of heaven, I pray it doesn't.

Georgie frowns over at the two blondes cuddling up to Warwick. "Justin Bieber just walked in and announced that he's looking for a couple of golden-haired cuties to put in his next video. And he's giving out free candy canes, too!"

"I'm a golden-haired cutie!" The one on the right takes off in a blur.

"How I'd love to take a bite out of his candy cane." The girl on the left zips off so fast Warwick's head is left on a swivel.

Georgie and I plant ourselves on their stools, and my seat has been nicely warmed for me.

"Well hello, ladies." Warwick chuckles as he looks from Georgie to me, and I can't help but chuckle back as I take him in with those reindeer antlers jingling softly on his head and that red plastic nose. "I can scoot over one so the two of you can sit together if you like?"

Georgie balks at the idea, "Why would I want to sit with her when I can sit next to you?" Her head does an odd wobble as she gives his beard a pinch. "Have I ever told you I've got a weakness for men with a good Vandyke?"

A warm laugh expels from him. "A woman who knows her beards. Please allow me to buy you a drink. I'm afraid we haven't met before." He holds a hand out her way. "Warwick Tully."

"Sounds to me as if we've been wasting time. With a beard like that, I bet you play an instrument, too. Let me guess, the tuba?"

He belts out a full-bellied laugh. "Close. Saxophone. What's your name, hot stuff?"

Saxophone. I avert my eyes a moment. I dated a guy once in college who played the sax and he almost ripped my head off when I dared to touch it. He let me know the brass is sensitive to the oil from people's fingertips. Turns out, I was sensitive to people almost ripping my head off and we parted ways soon thereafter.

"Georgie Conner, superfan of fuzzy faces the world over. And that's my keeper, Bizzy." She makes a face my way, but I'm thankful she's chosen to include me in her intro. Once Georgie starts to dominate a conversation, trying to interject is like trying to stick a post in dry cement.

Warwick inches back as he turns to examine me. "Bizzy? Is that you?" Another warm laugh strums from him.

I pull my nose off momentarily. "The one and only. But just between you and me, I'm really digging the disguise. I might just wear it around the inn for the rest of the month."

"You'll catch an eye or two." He gives a friendly wink. "What brings you out this way?"

I wonder if this has anything to do with the reading of the will? Would Joe have contacted her?

I nod out of reflex. I did receive a phone call from Joseph Goodyear, Quinn's attorney. He officially requested I be in the room during the reading of the will. He tipped me off and said that Quinn had some kind sentiments toward me and a special message. I can't wait to hear it. Even though we weren't terribly close, I really do miss him.

"Actually—" I glance back to the dance floor where a crowd has gathered around that keg once again. Only this time it's not Macy doing a handstand while having hops and barley shot into her mouth. It's Juni. A girl in a Dexter sweatshirt strides by and that's my cue. "I went to Dexter." I shrug over at him. "The alumni are always invited to these kinds of event. I was the official monitor of my dorm." True story.

Georgie pretends to retch. "That's code for tattletale." She rolls her eyes at him. "I bet that's where she got the nickname Buzzkill Bizzy."

"That is not my nickname," I'm quick to refute the less than fun-loving moniker.

"So she says." Georgie elbows him. "Don't listen to her. Once Bizzy Baker Wilder heads into the room, the fun-o'-meter starts to spin in the wrong direction." She leans a notch closer to him. "Don't tell her I said this—they don't exactly send her any invites to these shindigs. But you know how it goes, it's hard to keep the party police off the scene of the crime."

A robust laugh bucks from him. "Oh, I've known a few people like that."

The bartender comes by, and Warwick has us each order up a drink.

"Make mine a virgin," I say. "I'm driving."

"Make mine a double," Georgie calls out. "I'm having my good time and hers." She gives Warwick's beard a quick tickle. "And if you play your cards right, we can have a good time ourselves. I've got a cache of chocolate chip cookies back at my place and a bottle of moonshine I bought out of the trunk of some guy's car down in Edison last week."

"Georgie," I say as I shake my head at her. "That's illegal and probably deadly. When did you pick this up?"

"While you were showing off your stems in the kick line. You're not the only one who knows how to break a rule now and then. Besides, Christmas is coming right up. I've got a naughty list to make my way onto. I had to start somewhere. Don't worry, Biz. You might just find a bottle of white lightning under the tree on the big day yourself. He was running a special, and I needed to do a little Christmas shopping. He needed cash, and I needed a gift that would keep on giving. Talk about right place, right time." Her fingers walk up Warwick's arm. "Sort of like now."

Warwick nuzzles his nose her way, and my jaw goes slack.

Has she lost her mind? She does realize this is my rodeo, right?

"Don't listen to her, Warwick," I say. "If you play your cards wrong, they'll be hauling you out of her cottage in a few hours, unconscious. And there's a very good chance you won't wake up after she gives you that rat poison."

He shakes his head as a silent laugh bumps through his chest.

"You girls are a hoot." He pauses a moment as he looks my way. "Wait a minute. Did she say your surname was Wilder? As in *Detective* Wilder?"

Great.

"Yes, actually." I sigh because in the past, any mention of Jasper has even the most innocent of people clamming up. "We just got married this past September."

"Well, congratulations. Is there any news on the case? I can't believe someone would so brazenly do something like this." **Brazen is as brazen does.**

"No word. I was hoping they'd solve this before Christmas, but the holiday is just about here and the case is growing colder by the day." I don't dare tell him what I learned about Arthur. "Did you happen to see Quinn after the show? I mean, I'm not implicating you." I laugh at the thought. "But he must have had a disagreement with someone. That axe was a part of the show. Whoever did the deed acted out of spontaneous anger. Or at least that's what it looks like."

He nods. "I thought the same thing." He takes a deep breath. "You know, I had been thinking about it. Actually, I can't stop. Quinn was my very good friend. We did everything together. I used to call him my partner in crime. We started a business way back when, and it took off like wildfire. He was my good luck charm in every way. I wouldn't be the man I am today without him." **Isn't that the truth?**

I'm about to ask about his business when he lifts a finger in the air.

"There is something that I neglected to tell the detectives that night," he offers. "In fact, I planned on giving your husband a call. I didn't think it was important at the time, but I saw Quinn head out to the garden. I was heading out to speak with him myself, but I ended up stopping by the refreshment table and ate my weight in chocolate chip cookies and peppermint bark. Not an easy feat by any measure." His chest shakes as he swallows down a laugh. "I had to apologize to the cute brunette who works for you for making her job so hard when she came back to replenish the supply." **Lord knows I've got the belly to prove I have a sweet tooth.**

"Well, don't keep me in suspense," I whisper as I move to the edge of my seat. "What did you see that you're going to report to my husband? I mean, if you're comfortable sharing." Please, let him be comfortable sharing. It's not fair that Jasper gets all of the good stuff effortlessly and I have to listen to Georgie berate me to do it.

He takes a quick breath just as the bartender slides a couple of drinks over.

"On my tab." Warwick nods to the man. **After all, I'm assuming I'm the new owner.** His cheek flickers as if he wasn't sure how he felt about that. "Anyway, I finally made my way outside and saw Quinn and his accountant going at it."

"Arthur Silver?" My heart booms in my chest. I bet he got his own heart pumping after whacking poor Quinn to death. No wonder he took Macy up on her saucy offer. He wanted to get it off his mind while working out all that adrenaline that was coursing through his system.

"That's him." Warwick runs his finger around the lip of his glass. "Arthur was howling at the guy or I would have gone over. I stepped into the shadows for a moment, I'm ashamed to say, to hear what all the ruckus was about, but all I could make out was that Arthur wanted some money to pay his bills—Arthur's bills. Quinn always settled his own debts. No bill was ever late. For as wild as Quinn was with the women, he was a perfect square when it came to paying his bills on time and paying his taxes." **Too much of a square if you ask me. One with four sharp corners with which you could cut yourself.** He shakes his head. "Quinn said something back to him, calmly, of course. The man never raised his voice, and no sooner did Arthur take off than one of his old flames, Angelica Chatfield, came out."

"Angelica?" My head ticks to the side. "She's the socialite he said always knew how to bring men to their feet. I'm assuming because she has the voice of an angel. She gave a great performance that night." And she called Quinn's lawyer regarding the reading of the will before they hauled his body out of there, too, but I keep that nasty bit to myself.

"I don't know if I'd call her a socialite." His eyes flit to the ceiling. "Maybe she qualified, once upon a *dime*. But the woman is broke—has been for a couple of years. She's still keeping appearances, though."

A thought I intercepted from Angelica comes back to me. I distinctly remember her saying something to the effect that it was difficult maintaining her lifestyle. And now I know why.

"No kidding?" Georgie bleats. "How did she lose her money? Let me guess, she got robbed by the one-armed bandit. It happens to the best of us." She plucks the cherry out of her fruity drink and takes an angry bite.

Warwick chuckles. "I think a few bad investments had something to do with it. She bought up too much too fast—that real estate bubble a few years back didn't work in her favor either. And I seem to recall she liked to spend freely. People are surprised at how fast money can burn. Even the rich can find themselves in a predicament. I'm no billionaire, but I lost out on an investment myself about two years ago. I bought in on a few Donut Dungeons as a franchisee, and it turns out, the corporation sold me all of their dogs. I should have done my due diligence, but I'm afraid the only research I did was picking up a few too many boxes of crullers. Anyway, I had to do a little tap dancing, but I got out by the skin of my teeth. I'm not getting back into the food game anytime soon, that's for sure."

And that's exactly why I'm hoping Quinn didn't gift this place to me. Although knowing Quinn, he did it just to get a laugh out of it. Who knows? Maybe I can make this one work.

I lean in. " Did you happen to hear what Quinn and Angelica were talking about that night?"

He winces. "She was sharp-tongued. Called him every name in the book. Nothing I'd repeat with a couple of nice girls like you sitting by my side."

"He called me a girl." Georgie winks my way, and I choose to ignore it.

"And did Angelica leave upset?" I ask.

He shakes his head. "I left. I figured poor Quinn needed a moment to lick his wounds."

Georgie snaps her fingers. "So it was Angelica who did it. Knew it." She slaps her hand onto the counter. "It's always the ex-socialite. I bet she asked for cash and he pulled out the wrong bill. No wonder she hacked his hand off."

"*Georgie.*" I wrinkle my nose at her.

"Oh, it's true, Bizzy." Georgie shakes her head. "You've never seen anything like a socialite scorned. How do you think I got this scar?" She points to the cleft in her chin, and I make a face because I have a feeling we've just careened out of reality and into the magical land where Georgie's mind believes whatever comes out of her mouth—and as long as Warwick believes it, I don't mind one bit. "I was hunting sea glass down at Bar Harbor, and a rich witch tried to shake me down. And when I wouldn't hand over all my tumbled sea jewels, she pulled a blade on me." **How am I doing, kid?** Her eyes expand my way, and I shake my head at her. Georgie waves me off. "Anyway, this case is officially closed. I'm sure they'll cuff her tomorrow." She snuggles up next to Warwick. "You know what's not closed? My bedroom door. I'm the last cottage just past the inn. I'll leave a trail of chocolate chip cookies in case you have a hard time finding it."

The two of them share a throaty laugh, and I can't help but shake my head at it.

"She's clearly kidding," I say.

"I'm as serious as that heart attack I'm looking to give you." She blows the man a kiss before diving in for the real deal.

"Would you look at that"—I say, pulling Georgie off the stool—"the keg is free, and it's been years since either of us has done a decent handstand. It was nice talking to you, Warwick! I'll see you at the reading of the will!"

"Speak for yourself, sister," Georgie says as she tries to swat me off of her by way of her purse. But it's too late. I've dragged us over to beer central in hopes to herd Juni and Macy back to the car. I'll have to text Jasper and tell him not to bother to show. I've got everything we need.

Before I know what's happening, Macy and Juni storm me with a group of frat boys, chanting the words *chug it* over and over again. Someone lifts my legs off the ground and I grab onto the lip of the keg for dear life.

A perky brunette gives me a splash in the face with the spigot in her hand, and as I open my mouth to protest the effort, what feels like a gallon of beer is quickly funneled down my throat.

"GAH!" I twist my head to the side and end up giving myself a beer facial instead.

The next thing I know, I'm falling through the air before landing softly in the arms of a dangerously sexy, yet more than slightly bewildered homicide detective.

I take a moment to cringe. "Can you believe I wanted to see how limber I could be?"

He shakes his head, not a sign of a smile in sight.

"I can explain everything," I say the words in one quick breath before he decides to drop me like a stone and run for the hills. "Got a minute?"

"For you? I've got all night."

I collect my crime-fighting posse, and we hightail it back to Cider Cove.

And I spend all night explaining to Jasper everything I learned about Angelica and Arthur.

There is a very real possibility one of them took an axe to Quinn Bennet. But soon enough, we shelf all talk about the case, and I decide to test out how limber I can be in much more creative ways.

I leave on the reindeer antlers and blinking red nose to spice things up.

And yet, it's Jasper who slays me with his moves in the very best way.

"Here you go." Jordy lands a large plastic tub marked *Christmas* at my feet as I stand in front of a fresh evergreen the Sugar Plum Tree Lot just delivered. "The last of the Christmas ornaments. Are you sure we needed another tree?"

"Yes, we absolutely needed another tree. The reading of the will is tomorrow in the library, and I thought it would be a nice touch to have a tree in there. You know, get people's mind off the grief. And thank you for moving the tree from the entry to the library for me. I didn't think the tree lot was going to deliver a new one until tomorrow. At least this way the entry won't be bare."

"Oh yeah, it was fun shedding ornaments every two feet." He makes a face. Jordy looks exactly like Emmie in female skin—partially why that twenty-four hour marriage of ours didn't last. "But Sherlock helped pick them all up." He gives

Sherlock's ears a quick tussle. "I'll go finish up in the library. Just holler if you need me."

The inn is bustling, the snow is falling lightly outside, and I can see the flickering flames of the fireplace in the grand room. It's a perfect December afternoon, or at least it would be if Quinn Bennet's killer were behind bars. I can't believe the poor man was murdered, let alone right here at his own inn.

Fish mewls as she stretches her front paws and retracts her claws, one after the other. **Why do trees smell so good?**

So we know where to relieve ourselves! Rudolph gives an adorable little yip as he continues to run a circle around the evergreen. **Watch me do it now!**

"No, no, no," I say as sweetly yet sternly as I can. There's no way I can reprimand that cutie pie. He's far too adorable with the perennial smile on his face. It would be tantamount to yelling at a baby.

Sherlock gives a lazy bark. **Bizzy doesn't believe we should relieve ourselves indoors.**

Rudolph bites out a couple of cheery barks my way. **I've seen her do it!** His big brown eyes sparkle as he looks my way. **And I've caught Fish and Jasper doing it, too.**

"That's because we're not special enough to do our business outside," I'm quick to tell him in an effort to save my carpets.

Fish chirps, **Nor do we want to be.**

Rudolph runs right up to Fish and barks freely in her face. ***I'm not gonna be special then either.*** He runs to the base of the tree and lifts his leg.

"Don't you dare test me on this." It comes out a touch sterner than I intended, but once that little furry leg of his goes down, I know it was worth it.

Come on, kid. I'll take you outside. Sherlock nudges the little furball. ***I know how to open the door with my nose.***

They dart off just as Georgie hustles this way in one of her wonky quilt dresses that sports just about every holly jolly pattern.

"Where's the fire?" She stops short as they bullet past her. "Kids these days." She migrates my way and immediately gets to the task of putting ornaments on the tree. "Speaking of fire, I had a war with a well-lit wick in my cottage last night, if you know what I mean."

I take in a sharp breath. "Don't tell me that man took you up on your trail of chocolate chip cookies."

"Bizzy Baker Wilder," a deep voice belts out my name from behind, and I turn to see Leo Granger headed this way dressed in his olive-colored deputy duds with an ear-to-ear grin on his face.

He nods to Georgie. "Did I hear the words *trail of chocolate chip cookies*?"

"Yes," I snip, shooting the guilty party a look. "Georgie lured a man to her cottage by promising him carbs, sugar, and booze."

A husky laugh emits from her. "Oh, I made good on it, too—and then some."

Leo picks up a bright red ball of glass. "Can't say I blame the guy. You had me at cookies, Georgie."

"I had him, too." She gives a wistful shake of the head. "And I took bite after bite."

"Okay." I make eyes at Leo. "Guess what? I inadvertently pulled a little info out of my bestie. I know the perfect way you can propose."

Georgie scoffs. "Don't listen to her, Leo. Her marriage is on the rocks. She's forever sneaking off to bars looking for other men."

I avert my eyes. "Don't listen to the rumors, Leo. Jasper and I are fine. And those other men just so happen to be suspects."

"I saw Jasper this morning." He picks up another ornament. "He told me all about the keg-stand. Impressive. But Georgie's got a point. You're a married woman. I'd save the handstands for home. Just my humble opinion."

"I'll keep that in mind." I quickly fill him in on Emmie's dream proposal.

"That's great." He looks momentarily stunned. "Emmie always has a chocolate cake in the café. How about this— would you mind hiding the ring and serving the cake?"

"Done. Speaking of rings, did you decide which one to go with?"

He holds out his phone and pulls up a picture of a cushion cut diamond with a halo of smaller stones fringing it.

"Leo, it's perfect."

"*Mmm.*" Georgie melts as she takes it in. "Nothing says be mine forever than a compressed lump of coal. If she says no, I'm in."

"I might take you up on it." He slips his phone back into his pocket. "I'd better get back to work." He nods my way. "Jasper let me know forensics finally came back with the blood analysis."

"That's right," I say a little too giddy at the prospect. "Jasper was at the lab last night. He must have forgotten to mention the results when we got home."

Georgie clucks her tongue to Leo. "First, she's hanging out with frat boys in bars, and now he's keeping things from her. Got any single hot deputy friends lying around? *You-know-who* might be newly single soon herself." She ticks her head my way.

"Not true." I won't even entertain that nightmare.

Rudolph and Sherlock run back in just as Leo takes off, and Georgie and I finish decorating the tree.

Angelica Chatfield slipped something into Quinn's drink. She was the last person who spoke to him alive. I think the murderous math is beginning to add up, and it looks as if the sum total equals murder.

13

Diazepam.

Jasper filled me in on it last night as soon as he got home. In other words, *Valium* was found in Quinn's bloodstream. Not enough to kill him, just enough to make him weak. And on that white glove that was left at the scene, they found both Quinn's blood and chocolate. I guess the killer had a hankering for a sweet treat, not that I could blame them.

Emmie was at the helm of the refreshment table that night just like she is now in the library with me. The refreshment table looks just as delicious as the desserts with its bright red tablecloth and its festive looking poinsettia, each nestled in a fresh evergreen wreath.

"I still think Angelica was trying to drug him," I whisper to Jasper as Emmie and I put the last-minute touches on the refreshment table. Every inch of the library is gleaming with holiday perfection. The library is more of a formal sitting room with a few extra shelves of books. But the inn has a smaller lending library in the grand room as well. The fireplace is crackling, and the room holds the scent of the evergreen Jordy placed in the corner yesterday. I also had him fill the room with the ladderback chairs in a half-circle, ensconcing a desk that we turned to face the upcoming crowd. I have no idea how many to expect, but I put a couple of books on the seats off to the right of the desk where Jasper and I will sit. We made sure we'd have a full view of just about every face in here. It won't guarantee I'll be able to read their minds, but it will definitely up my odds. Jasper is the pro at reading faces. It'll help him, too.

"She might have been trying to drug him. It's a valid point." Jasper offers a sober nod while filling a Styrofoam cup with coffee. "If the guy was off his game, it certainly made it easier on the killer."

Emmie holds out a platter of sweets between us. "Cookie? Peppermint bark?"

"I'll never say no to that." I quickly swipe a snowball dusted with enough powdered sugar to build a snowman with and indulge in the buttery goodness.

"Chocolate chip for me," Jasper says, plucking one off the tray just as Emmie gasps.

"People are heading this way," she hisses in a panic. "I'm out of here." Emmie lands the platter on the table, and just as she skips on out, Georgie escorts in a tall, handsome man with an easy smile and a head full of gray hair.

Georgie holds a hand out my way and the sequins on her red kaftan sparkle like stars. "And this would be the manager at the inn, Bizzy Baker—Wilder. And her husband, Detective Wilder."

"Ah yes." The man's smile broadens. "Joseph Goodyear. I'm Quinn Bennet's attorney." He gives an affable nod. "As in present tense. That is, until the conclusion of today's proceedings." He strums a warm laugh. "It's great to meet you, Bizzy. You as well, Detective."

"Thank you," I say. "Is it okay that my husband is present? I was hoping he could be here—you know, for emotional support."

"Absolutely." He looks to Jasper. "I wouldn't take anyone off the suspect list just yet. Unfortunately, I've seen this play out before. The killer might just be in this very room today." **Quinn always said if he met an untimely demise that we wouldn't have to look far for the killer. I'd bet money he or she will be right in our midst today. I'll try to take a stab at who the killer might be myself. I've guessed correctly on a few occasions. Let's see if I can keep my track record going.** He nods as he begins to step away.

"Oh, and one more thing." I hold up my hand in an effort to stop him. "Would you mind extending an invitation to those that show up today to the Cider Cove Christmas Spectacular? It'll be right here on Main Street tomorrow evening. I know that won't help with the grief, but in the least they might have a little holiday magic to look forward to."

"It would be a delight." He gives a long blink as if to affirm it.

Georgie shudders. "Let's keep with the happy thoughts. How about I get you a cookie, hot shot? Chocolate chip?" she says those last two words low and throaty, and something tells me those cookies have been her seduction arsenal for quite some time. She leans my way and whispers, "Had I known I'd meet a king today I wouldn't have done the bad boogey with the pauper the other night."

Jasper's lids hood over, and he's looking at me with that glazed expression he gets right before things get interesting.

"What's that look for?" I tease.

"Let's just say that cookie worked up an appetite for something far sweeter." He lands a quick kiss to my lips. "I think we're both going to need a break after this."

"I so agree. Whatever shall we do?"

"The bad boogey," he says without missing a beat.

"I'll bring the chocolate chip cookies."

"You really know how to sweet talk a guy."

In an instant, the room fills with bodies. Georgie hightails it over to the legal eagle at the front of the room just as Eve French comes in with a modest black silk dress with red rhinestone buttons floating down the front. Her dark hair is pulled back into a bun, and she's wearing a dark chocolate brown lipstick that I only wish I could get away with.

"Bizzy." She offers a sorrowful smile. "We meet again."

"You look great. We have cookies and coffee set out. Please, help yourself."

"Ooh." She cranes her head past me. "I think I'll wait to indulge." She squints over to the attorney situating himself at the desk. ***Now there's the man of the hour. Let's hope he's about to hand the keys to the kingdom over today—right in my hands, that is.*** "Excuse me." She takes off just as the thick scent of cologne engulfs us, and in steps Arthur Silver.

He looks dapper in a dark suit, his face cleanly shaven.

"If it isn't the dancer." He gives a slight bow my way. "Nice to see you again, Bizzy. I suppose this is Quinn's last hurrah." His lips twitch as he looks to Eve speaking to Joseph. ***And there she is looking hotter than ever. Now that Quinn is gone, maybe I'll finally get my chance.*** "If you'll excuse me." He sheds an easy smile as he heads her way.

"He thinks he's got a chance with Eve," I whisper to Jasper, and his chest pumps with a quiet laugh.

"Funny. I was able to read his mind, too."

The door darkens and in strides Angelica with her blonde hair looking milky in the light and her dark-framed glasses accentuating her warm smile.

"Bizzy, nice to see you again." She pulls her coat tightly around her.

"Great to see you, too. If you give me your coat, I'll hang it for you."

"I'm fine. I have a feeling I'm going to want to make a quick escape." She shudders as she looks around. "The last time I was at one of these things, my father gave me the finger from the great beyond."

I grimace without meaning to, and she waves it off.

"I'm fine." A nervous titter escapes her. "So fine." She glowers toward Joseph Goodyear. ***This is your last chance to right all the wrongs, Quinn. Let's hope I don't have to wish you dead, twice.***

She takes off to find a seat, and Jasper leans in.

"Your mouth just fell open," he whispers. "Did we just get a confession?"

"Maybe."

"The party can start now," a voice bellows from the entry, and the entire room turns to see Warwick giving a jovial wave. He's dressed in a dark navy suit with a red and blue striped tie, and his beard is neatly trimmed to a point. And if I'm not mistaken, there seems to be a bounce to his step as he walks into the room. No doubt Georgie put it there.

I tip my head toward Jasper's and whisper, "That's the pauper Georgie was with the other night."

Jasper sighs as Warwick offers a nod and a wink our way before heading to the front of the class with the others.

Jasper and I take a seat to the right, and Georgie lands in the seat next to me.

"Get a load of this crowd, would you?" Georgie elbows me in the side. "That Judge Goodyear is a popular guy. With that full head of hair and mouth full of real teeth, who could blame every woman in this room for having hot fantasies about him?"

"He's the lawyer," I whisper. "And believe me, not a soul in this room is too concerned with him or his popularity. The only thing they care about is what he's about to say."

Something brushes against my ankles, and before I can look down, Fish jumps up in my lap.

I couldn't stay away, she mewls softly as she situates herself to face Joseph Goodyear along with the rest of us. *Don't worry about the tail waggers. Nessa and Grady have pulled out the tennis balls. I tried to warn them that you wouldn't like that, but they couldn't hear me with all the cheering, the barking, the running up and down the halls—the public urination.*

"Oh, for Pete's sake," I mutter a touch too loud, and the room quiets to a hush as they look my way.

Joseph Goodyear gives a light chuckle.

"And I agree." He nods my way. "It's time we move things along. First and foremost, thank you for being here today. I hope the holidays are treating you well. Bizzy, the inn looks like a quintessential holiday card. The tree, the refreshments, the dessert offerings—it's all far too kind. Your hospitality is impeccable. I can see now why Quinn regarded you so highly."

A tiny smile swims on my lips, and I give a little nod, acknowledging the sentiment.

"And on Bizzy's behalf, I'd like to extend an invitation to the Cider Cove Christmas Spectacular taking place tomorrow evening right here on Main Street. I think after something so tragic happens, it would be beneficial to feed your soul with something merry and bright. Now"—his voice grows sharp as he scans the crowd—"I'm going to start in the order that Quinn has outlined. I'm sure some of you are anxious to see where you fall in light of the fact Quinn was worth billions. Let us begin." He clears his throat and reads one by one the names of a few people I'm unfamiliar with, mostly friends or people he did business with. And he generously leaves them modest sums ranging from five thousand dollars to fifty. "Angelica Chatfield." He looks to the blonde who immediately spikes up in her seat. I can't blame her. I'd probably do the same. "To Angelica, my dear friend, I leave three payments of ten thousand dollars each—to be distributed one at a time in ten year increments."

Her eyes enlarge, and her lips knot up. **Bastard.**

She forces a smile. "Lovely." ***So much for quitting my day job. And now it's looking like I'll never leave the Davenport Steakhouse.*** Her fists clench. ***How I wish I could go back in time and kill him all over again.***

All over again? As in—she's done it once already?

The attorney's glasses slide down his nose as he leans toward the screen of his laptop.

"It says here, Angelica, I realize this isn't much, but it might be enough to bail you out every now and again. I fear should I leave you more than you can handle, you would immediately mismanage—"

"I'm well aware of the reasoning." She motions for him to continue. "Please, move on to someone else."

He does just that, knocking out a few more menial sums to people I don't know.

"Eve French?" He offers her a broad smile as she sits almost directly in front of him. "To my darling Eve, who was, in fact, the great love of my life. I owe you many apologies for ruining what could have been a blessed union between us. Contrary to what my appearances may have impressed, I do not have billions in liquidity, but I bequeath you the properties I own in England—one dusty castle and two country estates. I also give you a beach house I purchased stateside in Whaler's Cove knowing that some day it would be the home you and your precious Elsie would live in. In addition to this, I understand these properties could bring upon you financial duress, so I am leaving you my entire portfolio of financial investments, which include stocks, bonds, commodities, and cash of which were not distributed in the reading of my will."

A light gasp circles the room, and a cheer breaks out—from Georgie, of course, and I nudge her to stop.

Fish mewls, **There goes the beach house.**

Eve leans forward in her seat, her face pink with color.

"I don't know what to say." She gives a few rapid blinks. "I guess he loved me in his own way." **He loved me deeply. That means more to me than all the money in the world. But thankfully, he left more than enough of that, too. Goodbye, apartment. Beach house, here we come.**

Angelica snorts. "Wish he loved me a little better. I guess he preferred the cold fish routine."

Eve scoffs just as the attorney holds up a hand.

"Let's continue." He goes on with a couple more people before glancing to Arthur. "And to Arthur Silver, though you blamed me for much, I leave you great things. First, know this, you had no father—and the one the world almost provided next, you killed. Be it intentionally or unintentionally, I will never know your true heart regarding the matter. But in the days that we were getting to know one another, I decided to take you under my wing and made up my mind that I would be the father you needed. No, I did not lavish you with finances. I demanded you learn how to hustle, how to move, and claw your way to survival, and then to plenty. That being said, now that I am no longer here, I leave to you the Silver Collective in its entirety."

Arthur's chest expands like a wall, and his head ticks up a notch.

The attorney goes on. "Though I had a myriad of preventative measures in place in the event you decided to dip your hand into the trough, I will remove those constrictions.

This is now wholly your company, and my only hope is that you are mature enough to know that you worked for everything you have. You have learned the business inside and out, and it is entirely up to you if it grows. Be the man I always knew you could be. Enjoy this life, my son."

Arthur blows out a silent *thank you* to the ceiling. **Payday has come. And now I feel like a sack of trash for what transpired in the garden on that last night of his life.**

My lips part, and I shoot Jasper a look.

Another admission of guilt? Jasper's brows hike with his amusement, and I shrug as if to signify it might just be that.

"And then there is Warwick." The attorney broadens his smile in the direction of the jovial man himself. "To Warwick, my friend, my ally, and on occasion the enemy of both mine and yourself." A light titter circles the room. "I leave you Telenational in its entirety—including its Sky phones division, Sky Plus Provides, and small entities within the company."

"Telenational?" the word echoes around the room, and it even leaves my lips as I look to Jasper.

"Did you know Quinn owned Telenational?" I whisper his way.

Telenational is one of the biggest cell phone providers in this country. Jasper and I are on the plan, as is the inn. Not only that, but we both have the latest model Sky phones. Telenational rose to fame a couple of years ago when it was able to undercut its competitors' fees by half and now owns the lion's share of the telecommunications market.

He shakes his head with caution as I look back to the attorney.

"Warwick"—Joseph continues—"I only hope this is not to your detriment. There were words we shared regarding the corporation. I hope by the time this is revealed you have heeded them. Understand that with great power comes great responsibility—and you owe that responsibility first and foremost to yourself. Be wise. Be shrewd, but not to your own undoing. Have a wonderful life, my true friend."

"Bizzy"—Georgie pulls out her phone and holds it up to me—"I've got a Sky phone, and the thing is a piece of crap."

A laugh breaks out in the room, and Warwick raises his hand.

"Georgie, I'll personally be glad to look into any issues you're having with it," he volunteers with a grin.

"You bet, big boy," she says it in the sultriest voice she can muster, and another round of laughter ensues. "Expect a few chocolate chip cookies as payment—among other things."

"Georgie." I elbow her. "I thought you switched to the attorney," I whisper.

"Turns out, the pauper was the king just like in that story."

"The Prince and the Pauper." I nod her way. "Word of advice: Steer clear of royalty until we solve this homicide."

"Come to think about it, that man did have killer moves—in the bedroom."

Fish yowls, *Muzzle her, Bizzy.*

I'd rather have her committed.

The attorney looks around the room. "And there is one more disbursement left to detail. Bizzy Baker Wilder." He nods my way.

Disbursement? Fish's ears pique to attention, as do mine.

"Bizzy, my friend, my loyal employee, you have taken such good care of the Country Cottage Inn, it is safe to say you have treated it as if it were your own. Therefore, I bequeath to you the Country Cottage Inn itself along with the cottages and the acreages of land that it's settled on. However, it will be up to you to pay all necessary fees and logistics that go along with it. I hope that this is a blessing to you rather than a curse. I have instructed Arthur to continue aiding you in any manner possible. Cheers to you and cheers to all. Carry on now in this life. Smiles all around. Onward and forward."

The room breaks out into a microcosm of conversations all at once.

Georgie grips me and lets out a deafening moan of delight.

Jasper looks as if he's about to fall out of his seat.

Fish lets out a sharp mewl, *Bizzy, does this mean what I think it does?*

I nod blindly. "I think I just inherited the inn."

14

"You own the inn," Jasper says as he takes another bite out of a chocolate chip cookie.

"*We* own the inn," I counter as the two of us snuggle up on our sofa back at the cottage. The twinkle lights on the tree are flashing, but it's still bare of any ornaments. "The inn is ours. What's mine is yours, remember?"

Fish belts out a sharp meow from her perch on the sofa. **Don't forget about me. I've always suspected I owned this place.**

As soon as the reading of the will wrapped up, I asked Georgie not to breathe a word just yet regarding my newly acquired hunk of real estate. I snapped up a leftover platter of cookies and peppermint bark, and Jasper and I headed back to our cottage. Of course, not before we snapped up our menagerie, too.

Sherlock barks as Rudolph does his best to chew on his tail.

My tail is off-limits, kid. Sherlock tucks it between his legs in an effort to spare it from tiny teeth marks. ***Bizzy, you and Jasper need to think about putting in a twenty-four hour bacon bar.***

I chuckle as I quickly relay his comment to Jasper.

Jasper twitches his brows at his perpetually hungry pooch. "We'll take that into consideration." He looks my way. "I think that should be your new favorite catch phrase. I hate to break it to you, but that was the first in a very long list of requests you'll be fielding. Don't worry about a thing. Everything is perfect here just the way it is."

"I guess I'll need to have a staff meeting. A shakeup like this could prompt half of my employees to walk off the job—ironically because they fear that I'll give them the axe." I make a face at the dark analogy. I wouldn't be in this predicament if it weren't for an axe.

"Nobody is quitting because *you're* in charge." Jasper pulls me onto his lap. "If anything, they're going to be enthused to finally speak with the owner face to face. Quinn was a ghost to them from the beginning."

"Maybe so, but I need to reassure them that I'm not selling it or turning it into an unrecognizable version of itself. And I'll have to prove to them *and* myself that I can keep the cogs to the financial wheels turning. I mean, I see the bills. And I do try to keep electrical costs down. Just last year, I went through and replaced all of the light bulbs with those energy efficient ones, same with the toilets and showerheads. I've tried to keep costs down for Quinn because I was half-afraid if we drifted into the red he'd sell the place. And the inn really is my baby. Oh wow"—I look into Jasper's pale gray eyes—"it's really my baby now, isn't it? *Our* baby."

He gives a solemn nod. "And I promise you won't have to go it alone. What I would recommend is not making any immediate changes. Keep things status quo until you can come up for air."

"You're so right."

My phone pings, alerting me to a text message, and before I can pick it up off the table, it pings again and again.

"It's a text from Emmie," I say. "And Jordy, and Nessa, and Juni."

Jasper and I read them one by one.

Emmie—**CONGRATULATIONS! Just heard the news! OMGoodness. I'm so happy for you. When you get a chance, we should totally talk about replacing the café with an upscale bistro. I've got a ton of ideas for you!**

Jordy—**Awesome news. So happy for you. Now we can finally get that Olympic-size swimming pool we've been talking about.**

"The Olympic-size pool *we've* been talking about?" I balk. "I think the ocean is just fine. One less body of water for you to worry about."

Nessa—**Good for you, Bizzy! Grady and I are both doing a happy dance. Now we won't have to wait for Quinn to reply each time we ask for a raise.**

I cringe at that one. "There goes the excuse I had whenever anyone asked for more money."

Juni—**Mama just told me the good news, Biz! I guess this means you're buying dinner from here on out! Are you free tonight? Because I'm getting hungry!**

I sigh as I put down my phone. "Juni's right, I'll be buying dinner from here on out, but only because it's been a long-standing tradition whenever we're together."

Jasper buries a kiss next to my ear. "I can take you to dinner if you like."

"No, that's okay. And it's still early. I just want to clear my head a moment. What did you think of the behavior of those suspects at the reading?"

He blows a steady breath. "From what I could see only Angelica looked disappointed. Eve, well, she's pretty much set for life. And that smile she gave before she left let me know she was pretty thrilled. Arthur looked perplexed but elated. And Warwick definitely had a spring in his step."

"I didn't know Warwick was one of your suspects?"

"He is now that he acquired Telenational. Honestly, I think he got the biggest potential jackpot out of the deal. Outside of you, of course. I'll admit, I was a bit worried about the inn."

"Me too." I sigh with relief. "I guess it's all working out the way Quinn wanted. As for those suspects, well, their minds were prattling away today. Warwick was an open book. The guy didn't hold back his thoughts after the reading of the will. He was quite verbose when congratulating everyone. But Arthur seemed taken aback when he found out he was getting the Silver Collective in its entirety. He said that payday had come. And now he feels like a sack of trash for what transpired in the garden on that last night of Quinn's life. And then there was Eve. Her mind was filled with warm fuzzies and heart emojis. She said she knew he loved her deeply and that it meant more to her than all the money in the world."

He nods. "Warwick and Eve haven't given us anything to worry about—at least not according to their thoughts, but Arthur? He admitted to seeing Quinn in the garden that night—not to mention he admitted to having a heated exchange. He could have left and gotten the axe with which to kill Quinn. What about Angelica?"

"She was angry," I say. "Angelica said something to the effect that she wasn't able to quit her day job at the Davenport. Then she clenched her fists and said, 'How I wish I could go back in time and kill him all over again.'"

Jasper inches back. "Kill him all over again? *And* she was in the garden that night speaking to him?"

I nod. "Supposedly the last to speak to him."

Rudolph barks as he heads on over. *That must have been the lady I heard. I remember her saying something about a stingy beetle hole.*

I quickly relay it to Jasper, and my mouth twitches to the side. I think we both know she may have used another word outside of *beetle*.

Jasper scoops up Rudolph as he tries to jump onto the couch and I pull him onto my lap.

"What else do you remember, Rudolph?" I ask, playing with his silky soft ears. "Did you hear Quinn say anything back to her? Did he call for help or for her to *stop*?"

Rudolph gives another sharp bark. *I do remember something! She said, 'Next time I'll triple your dose,' and she walked away.*

I translate for Jasper. "Maybe she walked away to get the axe?"

He nods. "Maybe she did. I bet she's reeling with anger tonight." He tightens his arms around me, and Rudolph jumps to the floor once again and is back to chasing Sherlock. "How about we ditch work for the rest of the afternoon? I'll order in an early dinner to celebrate the inn, and we can decorate the tree and look up every bit of cyber information on the suspects at hand. I think if we put our heads together we can crack this case wide open."

"I thought you'd never ask."

Fish mewls, *Now that I've got an inn to run, I need to make sure my guests are safe, and that starts with catching whoever thought it was a good idea to commit a homicide right here on the grounds. I'm investigating with you.*

Sherlock barks. *I'll watch Rudolph. Bizzy, can you leave that animal channel on TV again? It really calms the little guy down.*

"You bet," I say, as I do just that. Jasper orders some Chinese food for us, and we get straight to the serious business of decorating that tree. A little mistletoe leads to a little kissing, and soon we're decorating each other with affection.

Suffice it to say, we choose to celebrate the right way.

15

The Cider Cove Christmas Spectacular has drawn in more residents and tourists alike than Cider Cove knows what to do with.

I'd bet good money all of Maine has drained into our cozy little town, with the exception of my handsome plus one. Jasper is still at the station, but as soon as he gets done, he's hightailing it this way. And I can't wait to take a sleigh ride with him. Kissing Jasper while gliding through the snow on a sleigh is exactly how I want this night to end. Hopefully, we'll have a little justice to go with it on the side.

It's a little after six in the evening, and the festivities are just getting underway. The overgrown tree at the end of Main Street is gleaming with thousands of twinkle lights and oversized ruby red ornaments strapped to its boughs. Garland and more twinkle lights are strung all up and down Main Street. There are cheerful wreaths with bright red bows dotted here and there while carolers stroll up and down the street belting out those cheery tunes we can't get enough of this time of year.

A couple of refreshment tables are set out laden with hot cocoa, an assortment of cookies, and peppermint bark. We have Santa and his elves, along with a mile long line of kids all waiting for a turn on the big guy's lap, but the star of the show is the snow. A fresh dusting fell over our world last night, which makes for the perfect backdrop for this Christmas Spectacular.

I've got Fish with me in the baby sling that she loves to nestle in whenever she's in it, and I'm glad about it, because on a night like tonight, I can use all the warmth this little inferno is willing to give me. Both Sherlock and Rudolph are with me as well, and I've spent the better part of an hour trying to detangle myself from the literal binds that Rudolph has caused with his enthusiasm to walk on the *white stuff*. It's safe to say we've still got some work to do with leash training.

The shops are brimming with customers—some more than others, and I can't help but hold Fish a little bit tighter as I see Macy storm out of Lather and Light with a look of fury.

"Bizzy Baker"—she snips as she pulls her coat tightly—"was that quilt chop shop your big idea?"

"No to both. I'm Bizzy Baker *Wilder*. And I don't think they're actually making quilts in there, so the phrase *chop shop* doesn't quite work either. But good effort on your part."

"Do you know what else is a good effort on my part? Running my business. Do you know what's not a good effort on my part? Sales. Those *two old broads* have stolen all of my customers. And don't for a second buy that dumb luck spiel they've been trying to feed me all week. This is a strategic takedown of my finances, one sale at a time." She storms in the direction of their business, and I follow along as we narrowly miss getting run over by one of the many sleighs that has been giving people a holiday thrill as they ride up and down the street. But just as Macy sails through the bright red doors, a familiar scowl is shed my way by none other than the woman of the hour.

"Mayor Woods." I offer a nod her way. "You really know how to throw a party. Everything is amazing."

She waves the idea off. "Never mind this ice spectacle. I have a proposal to tend to tomorrow night. I just picked up a titanium band at the jewelers and gave your mother back his class ring. So what have you come up with?"

"A bar brawl?" I tease. Although it is a play on Juni's fight night idea.

"A bar brawl?" She gives a lone blink. "Wait a minute..."

"No," I say emphatically. "No brawls. I'm hosting dinner at the inn."

Her lips crimp. "Your shiny new inn. I'd be a smidge envious, but then I'm getting a shiny new husband. The only boy I've ever wanted will finally be mine."

"The only boy you ever wanted?" My heart sinks. "I didn't know that, Mack. You never said anything all those years we were close."

"And have you or Emmie hold it over me? Please. I knew better than that." She gives a quick glance around at the festivities. "So what else do you got? I need to get going. This night isn't going to run itself. I have to mingle." She pulls her navy wool coat tightly and snarls at Fish.

"How about a walk in the snow under the moonlight? You could ask him by the water? The cove is beautiful this time of year with the moon dancing over it."

She makes a face. "Too soft. Too generic. Too similar to your own proposal."

"Jasper proposed in the gazebo."

"Next to the beach while the moon danced on the water." She sticks her finger down her throat and pretends to gag. "I'll go with option one." Her lips stretch into something vaguely like a smile as she looks to the crowd. "Come hell or high water, tomorrow night—I'm going to be an engaged woman." She stalks off before I can stop her.

"Wait, option one? The fight?" I ask, shaking my head down at the furry trio and the three of them whimper as if they were already terrified of the feisty exchange. Can't blame them. I am, too.

Inside of Two Old Broads, it's brightly lit with white twinkle lights lining all the shelves and counters on one side, and a haphazard string of large colorful lights strewn in a crooked pattern on the other. The right side is neat and orderly, as opposed to the left side of the store, which has clothes and quilts mixed onto tables and a pile of what looks to be some of Georgie's vases, trivets, and other mosaics on the floor.

The right side has a chalkboard sign over it that reads in a pleasant script font *Ree's Priceless Picks!* And the left side has a sign created out of sea glass embedded in grout that reads *Georgie's Junk. Get it while it's hot!*

The cheery sound of "Jingle Bell Rock" blares over the speakers, and if I'm not mistaken, the scent of chocolate chip cookies fills the air. Women and men alike are snapping up wonky quilts, wonky jackets, and wonky dresses. Even the wonky quilt bedding for pets is flying off the shelves.

We thread our way through the crowd until we hit the front registers where Mom, Georgie, and Juni are taking care of customers while wearing Santa hats with oversized elf ears attached to them. It's a comical sight, and even Fish is braying out a laugh at the three of them.

"Say cheese," Macy sings their way as she quickly snaps a picture. "As your web designer, I'll be sure to update your homepage and your bio pics."

Mom grunts as she looks to Georgie, "I told you she wasn't through humiliating us."

Georgie gives my sister the stink eye. "Go ahead and do it, missy. And just you wait. We'll be more popular than ever—with the men."

Macy gasps because, let's face it, Georgie hit her where it hurts.

Mom chuckles as she makes her way over to us. "Don't worry, Macy. We'll send our surplus of freaks from the North Pole your way." She pulls me into a hug. "Congratulations, Bizzy. Georgie just told me the good news. I can't believe you didn't call me yesterday when you found out."

Georgie comes over, and it's only then I note they're both wearing frilly red and white aprons ala Mrs. Claus over a wonky quilt dress.

Macy gags my way. "Are you knocked up already?"

"What? No!"

Sherlock barks. ***I heard Jasper say there would be lots of practice before he knocked you up.***

Rudolph gives a few yipes. ***What's knocked up?***

Fish mewls, ***Does this have anything to do with Sherlock knocking his tail against your bedroom door at night, demanding to be let in?***

I shake my head her way.

Mom laughs. "Bizzy! Have you swallowed the watermelon seed already?"

"No," I say it emphatically this time.

Watermelon! Fish perks up. ***Can you grow those inside of you, Bizzy?***

Sherlock barks. ***Watermelon is almost as good as bacon. Just wait until you try it, kiddo.*** He nudges Rudolph with his nose.

If it doesn't taste like bacon, I don't want it. Rudolph belts out an adorable *woof* while sniffing the wonky quilt Georgie has donned—no doubt looking for his favorite culinary treat. We've ruined him as far as kibble goes. Dinnertime has been pretty much a disaster as of late.

"No watermelon here." I look to Macy. "Quinn left me the inn."

Hux pops up behind my mother. "I heard the news, sis. Mackenzie told me. It's all over town. Congrats, Biz. I officially volunteer as your legal counsel. You'll be needing it."

"Thank you," I say. "I especially like the volunteer part."

Hux lifts a finger. "Let's not get carried away."

Macy steps forward. "Wait a minute. You're saying that earl who was killed left that entire property to you? Just like that?"

"Just like that." I nod. "There's a bit of paperwork to sift through, but it's mine to do as I wish—and I wish to keep the guests coming. It's all on me now if it sinks or floats."

Mom ticks her head. "It was sort of *on you* beforehand, too."

Fish yowls, ***And that's the only reason it's still floating today.***

I land a quick kiss to her forehead. She's not wrong.

Hux nods me over to the side, and we drift off as Georgie and Mom get back behind the registers. Macy snaps up a few chocolate chip cookies before joining us.

"It's all a go for tomorrow night." He gives a solemn nod my way. "I have the ring, a surefire way to tick her off, and the exact words I want to say once I drop to one knee. I just need to know where to do the deed."

"Oh wow," Macy says through a mouthful. "You're looking to do the deed with the monster mayor, aren't you?"

"Yup." He sheds a boyish grin. "You know what they say. Fourth time's the charm."

Macy cocks her head. "They also say you were a fool then and you're an older fool now."

"Mark Twain." I shrug over at my brother.

"Don't quote Twain to me." He frowns over at Macy. "Where's the family meeting up for the big day?"

"My place." I bounce on my feet. "I figured what better way to celebrate Christmas than at my very own inn." I bite down over a smile while I continue to bounce. I can't help it. The fact Quinn actually left me the inn is finally beginning to set in, and I'm starting to get giddy—or slap happy, most likely an unhealthy combo of both.

Macy scoffs. "I liked you better when I thought you were knocked up. Fine, I'll be there." She looks at Hux. "A fight *and* a proposal? There's no way I'm missing the fireworks." She starts to take off. "Stop over at my place, Bizzy. Maybe some of that ridiculous good luck of yours will rub off on me. You get a man with the ability to cuff you nightly, and an entire inn? I'm suing," she shouts as she drifts in the crowd.

"On what grounds?" I shout back.

"Stealing my wildest dreams and making them your own."

Hux shrugs. "She could have a case. You never know, she could win." He lifts his chin toward the crowd. "I'd better find something for Mackenzie. Any idea of what she might like?"

I'd point out that he was the one about to get on bended knee, he should know her best, but decided against it. If they do get hitched, it'll probably be a good thing that he doesn't scratch too much beneath the surface.

"Those wonky quilt dresses are a pretty hot commodity."

Fish meows as she playfully swipes the air up at my brother. ***Don't let him do it, Bizzy. Mayor Woods will chop his head off if he gifts her that thing, and I rather like his head attached to his body. Nobody takes a blade to my Uncle Hux.***

Sherlock whimpers, ***Mayor Woods has threatened to chop my tail off one too many times. I wouldn't trust her with a knife, Bizzy.***

Hux reaches down and gives Sherlock a quick pat before picking up Rudolph.

"Maybe I'll just give her this cute little fuzzball."

Rudolph yelps and jerks until he wiggles his way back to the floor.

I don't wanna get my tail cut off! Or my head! Save me, Sherlock! He nestles under Sherlock's paws in an effort to hide from Mackenzie's clutches.

I can't blame him.

"I doubt Mack's ready for a puppy," I say. "Let's have her get used to picking up after you first."

"Good idea. I'll go with the weird dress. See you tomorrow night. I'll be at the inn with my ring at the ready—and a fight. I've got a way to juice her up and good. I might need gloves."

"And a helmet." I frown as he takes off to find the perfect gift Mackenzie will never wear.

I'm about to head over and invite Georgie, Juni, and my mother to the inn tomorrow night when I spot a barrel-chested man with a bushy beard holding up a wonky quilt and looking at it as if he were trying to make heads or tails out of it.

"Ooh, let's go," I whisper to Sherlock and Rudolph as I navigate them that way. "Warwick Tully," I practically sing his name. Last night when Jasper and I did a cyber deep dive into each of the suspects, we were most impressed with Warwick. It turns out, he's been the acting CEO of Telenational for years now and has turned a virtually unknown, and on the verge of bankruptcy, company into a corporate giant overnight. It's remarkable what he's been able to do.

"Bizzy." He gives an open-mouthed smile as he looks my way and gives Fish a quick pat on the back. "Fancy meeting you here. I'm a bit deficient on gifts." He holds up the red and green wonky quilt my way. "I'm afraid my mother would love this."

We share a warm laugh. "I'm sure she'll love it. And if she doesn't, they've got a great return policy."

"Good to know. I might be rolling in the green, but it doesn't mean I like to part with it so quickly."

"Congratulations on Telenational. You're really incredible. What's your secret? I'd love to make the inn sparkle and shine financially—not that it wasn't before." Great way to make it seem as if I was doing just enough to get by when it belonged to Quinn. I've poured my heart and soul into that inn. But that doesn't mean I would turn down any advice he might have to offer.

He gives a knowing nod. "My suggestion is to give the people what they want. Raise the prices by double, and sell yourself as the biggest deal this side of Maine. Trust me, they'll come in droves."

"Wow, *double*?" I blink back. "I get the feeling the inn game is a lot different than the telecommunications game. I'm guessing it's like juxtaposing hopscotch to major league football."

He barks out a laugh. "That's great. But remember this, there's no business too small to capitalize off of a little creative branding." He gives a wink. "Have a great night, Bizzy. And Merry Christmas."

"Merry Christmas to you," I say as I make my way out of the melee and straight into a body. "Eve!" I stumble back after smacking right into her. "I'm so sorry."

"No worries. It's a zoo out tonight." The pretty brunette blinks back with her mini me in tow, and her daughter wastes no time in picking up Rudolph.

"Here's my baby." She gives him an enthused snuggle before she looks my way. "You do realize that I plan on kidnapping him one day soon, right?"

Fish mewls sharply at her, **Nobody touches my rambunctious little runt.**

Eve shakes her head. "Excuse her, Bizzy. I promise you, I didn't raise a dognapper."

"Not to worry." I drop a kiss to Fish's ear because I meant it just as much for her. "How are you doing? Has it sunk in yet that Quinn gave you so much? And those kind words. Clearly he loved you."

Tears come to her eyes instantly. "I don't think it will ever sink in. But we're excited."

"Especially about the beach house," Elsie adds. "And about dinner tomorrow night at the inn."

"Oh"—Eve holds out a hand—"I hope you don't mind. Macy just extended the invite."

I spot Arthur across the street speaking to Macy right this very minute.

"No, not at all," I tell her. "In fact, I look forward to seeing you both there."

Elsie hands Rudolph to me. "I can't wait. Just spending Christmas Eve with my sweet Ruddy will be a present in and of itself." She shoots a glance to her mother. "But not the only gift of the day."

I give a little laugh. "Enjoy the rest of the night. I'll see you both tomorrow."

A crowd bustles past me, and by the time I thread my way through it, Macy is back in her shop and Arthur is walking up the street.

"Arthur," I call after him, and he turns my way.

"Hey, Bizzy." He gives a wistful tick of the head as he quickly gives both Rudolph and Sherlock a scratch behind the ears. He's wrapped in a plaid jacket and has a thick green scarf bundled around his neck, making him look perfectly cozy for the frosty weather. "Congratulations on getting the inn. You must be thrilled. I'll keep the account with my company going for as long as you like. And if you have any questions, feel free to contact me. I'm pulling for you." He dots Fish's nose with his finger.

"Thank you, I really appreciate that. And I think I just saw you speaking to my sister."

"Tracy?"—he winces—"I mean Macy. I guess I misunderstood her the night we met." **Or she wanted to give me an alias, and I couldn't blame her for that.** "Anyway, I hope it's all right, but Macy just invited me to the inn for dinner tomorrow night."

"It's more than all right. Can I ask you a question about Quinn?"

"Anything."

"That night he was killed, you were in the garden with him. Did you happen to mention that detail to the sheriff's department?"

He winces. "I think so? Honestly, I can't remember anymore. I was in shock that night. Like I said before, at the start of the evening I was angry with Quinn. The guy was squeezing me financially, and I was at a breaking point. And then I happened to bump into someone I really liked. After I had a few words with Quinn, I bumped into her again." He glances in the direction of Macy's shop. "Let's just say I thought the night was ending on a good note for me." *And personally, I'm glad I couldn't recall it at the time. The last thing I need is to be pinned for another murder I didn't commit. I hope whoever did this to him suffers just the way they made him suffer.*

I give a solemn nod.

And just like that, Arthur Silver, my sister's date for Christmas Eve dinner, is wiped off the suspect list. If he had said those words to me, I would have doubted him. But he said it with the utmost sincerity—to himself.

My head juts forward. "Did Quinn ever mention Angelica?"

He offers a vacant glance to the crowd. "He did. He said his job that night was to avoid her at every cost. She was costing him money. Quinn had a low tolerance for two things—breaking the law and money-sucking leeches. He strongly believed in people making their own way in this world and keeping it above board while doing so."

"He was a wise man. I wish I had saved some of the emails he sent me instead of deleting them. Looking back, they'd be invaluable to me now."

"I have full access to his email account. I have the login information if you want. He kept a log of his online access codes with me. Just let me know when and I'll shoot it over to you." His phone rings and he chuckles. "I'd better take this. I'll see you tomorrow night."

"Will do." I watch as he walks away and whispers my sister's name into the phone.

Figures. Macy is smitten and she can't go two minutes without talking to the guy.

I scan the crowd and see the very woman I was hoping to find standing near the refreshment tables just a few doors down and head on over.

The blonde with the dark-framed glasses looks my way just as she snaps up a piece of peppermint bark.

"It's not the holidays until I've had my fill of candy parading around as a cookie." She gives a jovial wink. "How are you doing, Bizzy? Excited about the inn?"

"I'm thrilled," I say as I examine Angelica Chatfield in this murderous new light. She's wrapped in a cheery red wool coat with a red and white striped scarf and it looks like the perfect Christmas pairing. "The inn was a nice surprise. You didn't seem too pleased with what he left you. I'm sorry about that."

She sighs as she blows a kiss to Fish.

"You win some, you lose some. I guess Quinn didn't owe me nothing." *He did, but saying it out loud makes me sound entitled. And so what if I do? Quinn was my best friend for a time. He knew I made bad choices with men, in business, and with my money. He had one job—to be there for me at every cost.*

Fish mewls her way, *She's the killer, isn't she, Bizzy?*

Rudolph gives a sharp bark. *It's the woman from the garden.*

My blood runs cold as Sherlock whimpers.

Where's Jasper? Sherlock barks. *We've gone down this road one too many times. I think we should call Jasper to the scene. All we've got to defend ourselves with is bacon.*

Fish yowls, *Bizzy doesn't have bacon. You're thinking of Georgie. But there are cookies nearby.*

I want a cookie! Rudolph chirps.

Angelica laughs. "My, you've got a rowdy bunch. Mind if I throw the dogs a chocolate chip cookie?"

"No thanks. Chocolate can actually kill them." Just like she killed Quinn. "Angelica, I know you were in the garden that night."

"No." She shakes her head, her eyes wide with horror. "I

wasn't in the garden. I swear it."

"We have a witness. Warwick saw you there. You were arguing with Quinn. There was physical evidence you were at the scene. There was a red crystal in the garden that night—the sheriff's department has it as evidence. It came off of your dress."

Her eyes close tightly and the peppermint bark snaps between her fingers.

"Angelica, I know that you've hit hard times," I say it softly. "That night you told me that it was exhausting to run in your socialite circles—and it's because it's taking all you've got to keep up appearances, isn't it? You've mismanaged your money, and you were trying to shake Quinn down that night for cash, weren't you?"

A fire ignites in her eyes. "So what if I was? So what if I lied about being in the garden that night? When they asked, I had no idea what that area was called. It was an innocent misstep on my part at first, but by then I didn't want to change my story. Who would? I've already got a major strike against me if anyone finds out I'm struggling—and they will. I don't exactly hide my employment. A few very important people I know have come by the Davenport Steakhouse. Word is already getting out." She glares at a horse-drawn sleigh as it zips on by, leaving the happy chime of bells in its wake. "Quinn knew if he left me any more money I would have squandered it." Her shoulders sag. "He would have been right."

"But he did leave you something. Maybe this will force

you to manage your money better. That's not a bad thing. Quinn didn't have to give you anything. And I'm betting that's what he was telling you in the garden that night when you struck him."

"Struck him?" She inches back.

I nod. "That's why you slipped some diazepam in his coffee earlier, isn't it? You wanted to weaken him?"

Both Rudolph and Sherlock growl in unison.

"Weaken him?" Her eyes spring wide open. "Bizzy, Quinn forgot to bring his anxiety medication. He emailed me earlier that day and asked if I would bring my own."

"Then why did you slip it into his drink when he wasn't looking?"

"He wasn't looking?" She looks almost as amused by my line of questioning as she does terrified. "Maybe he turned his head? Look, I'm not liking what you're implying. If Quinn had a bead on him from my dress, it's because he embraced me in the garden once we met up. And his anxiety is highly documented with his doctor, I'm sure—as is mine." ***For heaven's sake. And to think I came here to get my mind off of things.*** "I'm leaving now. Hopefully, the next time we meet, the killer will have been apprehended and you won't be moved to entertain such lunacy."

"Wait!" I call out after her. "What about the white glove?"

"I wouldn't be caught dead wearing white on any part of my body after September," she shouts back with a clear note of exasperation in her voice.

Fish growls, ***How dare she yell at you. And she's wearing a red and white scarf, isn't she?***

"She is, but I'll be the last person to point it out."

She stalks off just as the carolers stroll this way singing a cheerful rendition of "Rudolph the Red-Nosed Reindeer," and Rudolph jumps and dances once he hears his name.

Fish lands her paw over my chest. ***What do you think, Bizzy? Is she innocent or guilty?***

"I don't know," I whisper. "But I think there's a way to find out."

I text Arthur and ask if he can send me that access list to Quinn's email, and in less than a few seconds I have it.

My fingers work quickly as I pry into Quinn's account. If I can't read his mind, maybe I can read his emails. And sure enough, they populate my screen one by one. An exchange between Angelica and Quinn corroborates her claim. Quinn forgot his meds and wanted her to bring her own—stating he can't swallow pills. He requested capsules.

But I'm not deterred in the least about that, because it's what I find in Quinn's other email exchanges that sends a chill up my spine.

I glance up at my mother's shop across the way.

I know who the killer is.

16

Downtown Cider Cove has never felt so joyous, so merry and bright. It's almost seven in the evening, the carolers are belting out their spirited Christmas tunes, and the sound of bells chiming liven up the atmosphere with just the right measure of holiday cheer as the crowd grows thicker by the moment.

It takes a heroic effort to thread my way through the thicket of bodies as I head across the street to the shop where I last saw my one and only remaining suspect.

I'm about to step back into Two Old Broads when out bursts a man clad in a black wool coat, and Fish gives a rather aggressive meow his way—Warwick Tully.

"You play the saxophone," I say, breathless, and he gives a curious tilt of the head.

"Hey, Bizzy"—a small laugh bumps from him as we step off to the side to allow for the flow of shoppers elbowing their way into the shop—"that I do. Don't tell me the high school band needs someone to pinch-hit for them." He winces just as a sleigh full of screaming children flies by.

"No, I just remembered something. That night at the bistro, you had mentioned it to Georgie."

"Ah yes. She had thought I played the tuba. Not my style. Soprano sax is where I can really lose myself."

"Were you going to play for the showcase the night that Quinn died?"

"Actually, I was. One of the acts was running late, so Quinn had me bring my instrument. I've always got it with me in the trunk of the car regardless. You never know when the mood is going to strike."

Sherlock nudges my leg and gives a soft bark. ***Call Jasper, Bizzy. Don't do this.***

Do what? Rudolph's tail wags back and forth at supersonic speeds.

Fish mewls, ***Oh, for Pete's sake, Sherlock Bones, she's fine. Would you look at all the people here? What could possibly go wrong?***

My sentiments exactly. Or at least I'm hoping nothing goes wrong. Besides, I texted Jasper as I crossed the street and told him I needed him asap in front of my mother's shop. And lucky for me, that's exactly where I'm planted.

"No, the band is fine, I'm assuming." I try to muster a laugh but can't seem to initiate it. "I dated a guy once who played the sax. He really blew a gasket when I reached out to touch it one day."

"Oh, I get it. I never touch my girl with bare hands." A cheesy gurgle expels from him. "The brass can muck up pretty easily, and they are a beast to clean."

I nod. "And that's why he had a pair of thin white gloves in the case along with the instrument."

"A true musician after my own heart." He reaches into his pocket and produces a thin white glove—identical to the one I saw at the scene of the crime.

If the information I just gleaned from Quinn's emails is true, then he had a solid motive to want Quinn Bennet dead.

My breathing picks up as I examine the glowing glove.

Don't do it, Bizzy. Sherlock barks up at me.

"You don't have the other one, do you?" It comes out more of a fact than a question.

Sherlock whimpers, ***And here we go.***

Warwick's head hitches back a moment.

He checks his pocket for a moment before ceasing all movement.

Yes, the glove. He gives a long blink.

"I'm sorry, Bizzy. I have an engagement I need to get to." He tries to push past me, but I quickly hop in his path and both Sherlock and Rudolph growl and bark up at him.

"What's this?" A dull laugh pumps from him as he looks down at the two of them. "Easy, boys." He flashes a tight smile my way. "If I didn't know better, I'd think it was dinnertime." ***And I'm on the menu.*** He squints over at me. ***It looks as***

if I'm on Bizzy's menu as well—and she's hungry with suspicion.

And I have every reason to be.

"Warwick, you were in the garden that night with Quinn. In fact, you were the last to see him."

His eyes harden over mine. ***She can't prove it.***

I nod. "You were eating chocolate. The glove had both chocolate and Quinn's blood on it."

He cocks his head playfully. "But did it have mine?"

Fish yowls, ***He's got quite an attitude for a killer, hasn't he?***

I'd have to agree. But I have a feeling I know how to wipe that smug look off his face.

"You know, Warwick, one of the first things I heard Quinn say to you that day was regarding Telenational. He asked if you had the latest Sky phone for him." I nod.

"And I did." That came out of left field. "Sadly, I was unable to give it to him. Still have it, brand new in the box. Don't tell Georgie, but I thought she might like to find it in her stocking. We've got a hot date later." He gives a sly wink.

Fish mewls, ***Over my dead body. My claws have been itching to pluck out an eyeball or two. There's still time to get on Santa's naughty list yet.***

"I heard a little bit more of the conversation that night," I say as I harden my gaze over him.

"You were eavesdropping?" His face smooths out with amusement. ***I'm not about to be bested by an innkeeper.***

"No, not eavesdropping. You were having the conversation right in front of me. And then Quinn asked if you heeded his words. He was giving you advice, I take it?"

"When wasn't Quinn giving anyone advice?" His eyes flit to the crowd, and I can feel him plotting his escape.

"He was giving you advice on Telenational, wasn't he?"

"Telenational? Why yes. Were you looking for more business advice?" ***I can't get a read on this girl. She's all over the place. I never did understand women. I think it's time to cut my losses in Cider Cove. That's too bad. Georgie knew how to throw a hell of a party for two.***

"No." My mind swims with thoughts. "That night of the Christmas showcase, Quinn thanked you in front of the crowd. He said you were the sharpest knife in just about any room. He warned the audience not to turn their back on you or you just might cut them with it. And now I wonder if he meant that literally or figuratively." Obviously both.

His eyes round out.

"He was teasing, Bizzy. You can't be serious. I would never hurt a friend."

"But you did. Quinn didn't want you to taint Telenational's reputation any more than you did. He asked you to do the right thing. And you repaid him by going after him with an axe."

"Bizzy." He staggers back a few steps, looking genuinely stunned. "You can't prove it." *I have to get the hell out of here.* His eyes flit to the street once again.

"Yes, Warwick, I can. After you had the cookies that night, you went to get the axe, didn't you?"

"*Bizzy*, this is entirely out of your imagination." He takes another full step back toward the street, and I follow along.

"I should have known the day you came by to see the inn you weren't there to pay respects to Quinn. You were sizing up the inn because you thought it would land in your lap just like Telenational did."

His expression sours. "Indeed. I'm still baffled why he's given it to you. But I wish you and yours a merry Christmas."

He takes another step toward the street, and I throw myself in front of him once again.

"Telenational was a fledgling company when you took it on," I pant. "But you turned it around with misleading financial accounts. You exploited anyone and everyone who was willing to do business with you. There were so many schemes and scams you had running, I bet it took Quinn a while to catch on, but when he did, he was horrified. Quinn Bennet knew enough to stay above board when it came to business, and you were so far beneath it you might as well have been on the ocean floor. You established numerous limited liability special-purpose entities."

"Completely common in the telecommunications game."

"But perfectly illegal once you started using them to transfer some of your liabilities so they wouldn't appear in your account—therefore, allowing you to increase a robust stock price for the company, making it that much more appetizing to investors. It turns out, many of your recorded assets are inflated, aren't they, Warwick? And some are fraudulent or outright don't exist. More or less the exact advice you gave me when I asked how I could increase profits at the inn."

He searches my features as his lips part. **Quinn must have spoken with her. But why bring it up now? Something's not right.** "You have no proof."

"I do and so does the Seaview Sheriff's Department. I've forwarded the entire cache of Quinn's emails over to them. You'll be charged with illegal accounting practices, wire fraud, and who knows what else. The company will go bankrupt, as it was destined to do in the beginning. But that's the least of your worries. You killed Quinn, didn't you?" Fish's ear twitches as I ask the question, and both Sherlock and Rudolph sit rapt at attention.

His lips pull tightly. "Yes, I killed him, Bizzy." His eyes darken. "Quinn was a fool to think anyone's business acumen would be enough to save that money pit he acquired. I did what needed to be done. And when he discovered my tactics, he had the nerve to be outraged. I thought he'd be proud. And after a lengthy email exchange, he made the decision to fly out this way. It was his last-ditch effort to get me to comply or he'd rat me out himself. He didn't do it, Bizzy. I didn't give him the chance. But you did—you ratted me out." His expression goes cold as he walks my way, and I back up into the street until my knees get cut off and I fall backward into an empty sleigh.

Warwick covers my body with his own, and Fish lets out a wild screech as she struggles to get out from between us.

Sherlock barks as he hops into the sleigh, as does Rudolph, and the horse manning this wonder whinnies and hops back onto its hind legs before taking off with a start. The crowd screams with horror as the sleigh takes off down Main Street at horrific speeds.

"Perfect." Warwick gives an unsteady laugh as he looks down at me. "We'll make it look like an accident. You cracked your skull on a runaway sleigh. And I'll simply runaway." He clamps his hands around my neck and instantly I can't breathe.

My legs flail as my fingers struggle to pluck him off me.

Fish shrieks once again and wraps her entire body around his head, scratching and clawing in a fury.

Rudolph yipes and barks nonstop as he jumps over Warwick's back and starts biting his neck.

Don't worry, Bizzy. Sherlock lets out a ferocious bark. ***I know just what to do.*** He hops onto Warwick's back as well and Warwick's body crushes over mine that much more, but his hands are unrelenting in their pursuit.

Suddenly, Warwick's chest bucks as he lets out a horrific howl, and his hands release just enough for me to scoot back a good foot until my head hits the other side of the seat. It looks as if that skull cracker is still in the cards.

The sleigh bucks violently, and before I can process what's happening, Jasper's face appears above mine ever so briefly as he does his best to snatch the reins and grab onto Warwick at the very same time. The horse slows, and Jasper drops the reins long enough to bash Warwick's head into the side of the sleigh and cuff him.

And just like that, it's over.

"He did it," I pant. "He killed Quinn." I struggle to catch my breath as my hand claws at my neck. "And he almost killed me."

As soon as the sleigh rolls to a stop, Leo jumps in and pulls Warwick off. I catch a glance of the man's face, and it looks as if he's gone through a war.

"You really did a number on him," I say breathlessly as I pull Fish over to myself and kiss her. "Good work."

Jasper helps me sit up and wraps his arms around me while dropping a hot kiss onto my forehead. He pulls back as the snow falls gently between us.

"You have got to stop taking down suspects like that, Bizzy." His gray eyes shine like lightning in the night. "But I don't think you're going to." His lips flicker with a sad smile as he lands a kiss to my lips. "I love you, Bizzy Baker Wilder. You scare the hell out of me, but I love you."

And I show him exactly how much I love him without words.

Kissing Jasper in the snow while on a sleigh ride is exactly how I wanted this night to end—along with a little justice served up on the side.

And it looks as if I've gotten my wish.

When I was a child—and my family was still intact—Christmas Eve was a night filled with wonder for my brother, sister, and me.

My mother would read the Christmas story to us right out of the family Bible, and then my father would read *'Twas the Night Before Christmas.* My mother would gift us each brand new, warm and fresh from the dryer, matching Christmas pajamas, and we were quickly ushered off to bed.

But the three of us wouldn't dare fall asleep until we heard the sound of sleigh bells coming from the rooftop. Little did we know it was our father in the attic with a tambourine. There's so much magic and joy on Christmas Eve, I want to make sure I provide that for others on this special night. And seeing that I'll have a full house, or an inn full as it were, of family and friends—and three marriage proposals on the horizon— tonight needs to be perfect.

Not a single guest opted to dine in this evening; they all scattered to the four corners of Maine to celebrate with family. I let Nessa and Grady off work early, along with the rest of the staff, and Emmie helped prepare a feast from the Country Cottage Café. I stayed safely away from the kitchen as to not create a culinary disaster. Instead, Jordy helped me set up the formal dining room with a few conjoining tables, red tablecloths, gold runners, poinsettia centerpieces with evergreen boughs and candles, fine china, crystal goblets, and linen napkins. A stately tall blue noble stands proud in the corner, festooned from top to bottom with white twinkle lights and enough red ornaments to qualify as an apple tree. I wanted everything to be perfect. And it was—at least as far as dinner went.

But now dinner is over, the Christmas carols are a touch too loud, and the grand dining room is filled with lively conversations and laughter.

"Bizzy Bizzy." My father gives me a pat on the back. "You outdid yourself, kiddo. If you run out of room in the fridge for all those leftovers, I'll gladly take them off your hands." He pats his stomach, and I laugh.

"Don't worry, Dad. I made sure there would be plenty for anyone who wanted to take some food home. And don't forget the desserts." Emmie and Leo are still pulling out the pies, the cookies, and the mounds of peppermint bark. I told Leo he should keep her from indulging. I've hidden a slice of chocolate cake, filled with that platinum diamond ring he picked out, in the reception area in the mini fridge by my desk. And I need Emmie's sweet tooth to be revved up and ready to go when it's presented to her.

Gwyneth wraps her arms around Jasper. "Well, son, I can honestly say that you and your wife have been gracious hosts—and hosting us at your very own inn no less. I can't wait to tell all of my friends the good news."

Ever since Gwyneth found out the news about the inn, she's liked me just a little bit more. I'm not sure what that says—not great things. But at least now she finds me brag-worthy to her buddies. Baby steps. I'll take what I can get.

She scoots my father toward the dessert table.

"I see a pumpkin pie with my name on it," she purrs.

"I'm going for both that and the pecan," Dad is quick to warn her.

Jasper pulls me in and touches his nose to mine. "Fantastic." I take in his spiced cologne and hold it in my lungs a moment. Jasper looks like a delicious dream with his dark suit and slick red tie.

"Dinner? Or the fact I got all three of our fur babies to nestle by the fireplace?" Along with Fish, Sherlock Bones, and Rudolph, Emmie brought her dog, Cinnamon, a curly-haired labradoodle the exact color of her sweet name, and Gatsby, Leo's blond golden retriever, is here as well. They've kept us entertained for most of the evening. And all of them are wearing a bright red bow around their collar, giving them a festive appeal for the night.

He shakes his head. "You. You're a crime fighter by day, hostess with the mostess by night."

"Ooh, hostess with the mostess." I bite down on a flirty smile. "I do aim to please. Play your cards right, and I'll be taking those hosting skills of mine to the bedroom." Over his shoulder I spot Elsie, Eve French's daughter, cuddling up with Rudolph, and he's licking her face silly. "I take it back. Only two of our fur babies are by the fire. Elsie has really fallen in love with Rudolph, and I can tell he loves her, too."

Jasper takes a deep breath. "Are you willing to make a little girl's puppy Christmas wish come true?"

"Let's talk to Mom first." I wrinkle my nose as we head over to where Macy and Eve are having an animated conversation with Arthur Silver.

"Hey, hey"—Macy lifts her eggnog my way—"if it isn't the *Bizzy* bee herself. Great dinner. I'll be taking a pie to go."

"I expected nothing less." I laugh.

Arthur nods our way. "And good job to the two of you for bringing down Quinn's killer. I still can't believe it was Warwick." He shakes his head at the thought. "I guess you can never really know a person."

"Some people can surprise you," Jasper says. "I'm glad things are working out for you, though. And thank you for helping Bizzy with the accounting. We appreciate that."

Eve presses her lips tightly. "I was rooting for you, Bizzy. The night we were all here for the showcase and Quinn passed away, I thought about this beautiful inn. I really was hoping he would leave it to you. I'm glad to know Quinn did just that."

"Speaking of things that Quinn left..." I shrug. "You know, Elsie really seems to have taken to Rudolph. Would you, by chance, be open to welcoming a tiny furry cutie pie into the family?"

She sucks in a quick breath. "Yes!" She hoists both fists in the air and gives a victorious shake. "You bet I would! Oh, I can't wait to tell her. Can I tell her?"

"I'll go with you. I want to talk to Rudolph about it as well." I give her a little wink, even though I'm dead serious.

We head over, and Eve blurts it all out in one breath.

Elsie screams and jumps and gives poor Rudolph a good jostle in the process.

Rudolph gives a few happy yips. ***Is it true, Bizzy? Am I getting my very own family for Christmas?***

Fish runs over, as does Sherlock, both waiting with bated breath for my answer and I give a little nod.

"Are you okay with this, Rudolph?" I whisper, and he gives a sharp bark in return.

Yes!

Congratulations, Fish mewls. ***Do visit.***

Sherlock whimpers, ***I was just getting used to having you around. Make sure they give you lots of bacon, little guy.***

I give Rudolph a kiss on his forehead. "I'm happy for you—both." I look to Elsie. "Please stop by the inn often. We're going to miss him something awful."

"Are you kidding?" Her eyes grow wide. "This place is the *it* resort. You bet we're going to visit. Especially when it warms up. I love the cove."

Eve shrugs. "Then it's settled. You'll be seeing a lot of the three of us." She gives Rudolph a quick scratch and he licks her hand.

"Bizzy?" someone hisses from behind, and I see Mackenzie snarling while curling her finger as she calls me over.

"Excuse me," I say as I head her way. Mackenzie has her long chestnut hair perfectly coiled, a cranberry pantsuit on, and heels that even Macy would be envious of with their spiked metal heels. "Mayor Woods." I give a sly smile.

"Don't give me that Mayor Woods bull. I've got a titanium ring burning a hole in my pocket. "When should I initiate World War III?"

I make a face at her before glancing back at Emmie and Leo still tending to the dessert table. My brother isn't too far off as he stands speaking to Jasper and my father, looking relaxed, and satiated, and very much as if he forgot all about the next matrimonial blunder he was about to head into.

"Give it a couple of minutes," I say. "I'll pull him out of that conversation."

Georgie, Juni, my mother, and Macy all trot over, each in their Christmas finery. Both Georgie and Mom are wearing wonky quilt dresses in various patterns of red and green—a stark departure from my mother's typical preppy style, but she's made it clear she wants to represent the brand. And, of course, there's Macy in a red lacy dress that can double as lingerie.

Juni gives Mackenzie a few light taps on the face, just this side of a slap, and I hold my breath in the event Mack decides to start that bar brawl a little early.

Mack lifts her chin to Juni. "What do you want, simple one?"

"I'm tryin' to center ya. That's what a good coach does right before the big fight."

Mackenzie rolls her eyes. "It's nice to know at least you're on my side."

Georgie pokes her finger at Mack. "When's this going down, sister? I've got my camera poised and at the ready. I'll be taking the money shot, if you know what I mean."

"Yeah," Mom grunts a laugh. "She means she'll want money for it."

Mackenzie shrugs. "Take the right shot, and you just might get it."

A dark laugh springs from Macy. "And I'm taking Emmie's picture."

Mackenzie sucks in a quick breath. "What's this? Don't tell me the kitchen mouse is going for the gold tonight, too."

I straighten. "Call her a kitchen mouse again, and there will be a very real World War III on your hands."

"Fine." Her expression sours. "Just make sure we're not doing it right next to one another. I'll need some breathing room."

"Done," I say. "Give me five minutes."

I trot over to where Hux stands with my father and Jasper.

"Are you ready to fall on the sword?" I ask my brother, and he frowns over at me.

"Bizzy, this is a big night for me. I may not look it, but I'm nervous. Cut me a little slack. I can use your support."

"I'm sorry." I wince. "Let's just say I have it on good authority that everything works out in your favor. You have absolutely nothing to worry about."

Dad pats him on the back. "I think you have a solid plan, son. Start with a fight and end with a kiss. I've used that formula for years, and look where it's gotten me." He inches back. "Never mind. I have good faith it'll take you to a heck of a lot better than I did. This is the real deal. I can see it in your eyes. I can't wait to be the first to congratulate you."

Jasper leans in a notch. "Get your head in the game and speak from the heart."

"Oh, I will." Hux gurgles with a laugh.

Leo comes over, looking lean and mean in a dark inky suit. "Emmie is on her way back from the kitchen, last trip. I told her I'd eat dessert with her when she got back. It's go time, Bizzy."

"Great." I bounce on the balls of my feet, giddy for my bestie to finally get her moment. "I'll go get the cake." I take up Jasper's hand and mouth the words *come with me.*

We head into the foyer, and I pull him close. "Jasper, both Hux and Mackenzie have decided to go with a proposal that starts off as an argument."

A moaning sound comes from him. "Bizzy? Are you in any way responsible for the chaos that's about to ensue?"

I shake my head. "Someone far more creative than me."

He's right back to moaning.

I trot us over to my mini fridge and quickly shuttle that pricey piece of cake over to Leo.

His hands shake as he takes it and closes his eyes for a moment.

"Here it goes." He looks up at Jasper and me. "She's going to say yes, right?"

"Of course," I tell him. "And believe me, your proposal is going to take the cake." I give a little wink as Emmie walks back into the room. "Go, go—you're on," I whisper.

Leo strides over with the cake in hand, and Emmie coos at the sight of it.

The two of them head back to the table, and I'm about to wrap my arms around Jasper when Hux strides over.

"I'm going in," he whispers as he walks boldly over to the tree where Mackenzie stands alone as if priming herself for this moment, and I have no doubt she is.

"A double proposal." Jasper hugs me from behind as we enjoy a bird's-eye view of both happy couples. Across from us, Mom, Dad, Gwyneth, Jordy, Macy, Georgie, Juni, in addition to Eve, Elsie, and Arthur are at attention.

Emmie takes the first bite of that luscious layer chocolate cake, and I'm ready to drool for a bite myself.

Jasper tucks his mouth to my ear. "Where did you plant the ring?"

"About halfway in," I whisper.

Hux's voice hikes a notch from the tree, and I can see Mackenzie's cheeks pique with color.

"What are you talking about?" she practically shrieks. "Are you saying you're thinking of breaking up with me? *Here*? On Christmas Eve?"

"Yes," he belts it out. "That's exactly what I'm trying to tell you."

Georgie breaks out into spontaneous applause, and Mom nudges for her to stop.

"Ha!" Mackenzie laughs in my brother's face. "You wish you could break up with me. I was just about to break things off with you—only I had the class to wait until the new year. You are cold-blooded, Huxley Baker. And that's exactly why you'll spend the rest of your life in and out of dead-end marriages. You don't care about people. The only thing you care about is the chase. Well, guess what? I only care about the chase *myself*. And I'm all done chasing you." Her voice hikes to the ceiling, and the entire lot of us gasps.

Emmie bucks and garners my attention as her hand slips to her throat.

"Oh, here they go," I whisper with excitement as I pull Jasper around me tightly. "It's happening."

He nods. I'm not entirely sure if it's going as planned for Hux, but Emmie looks surprised, and Leo looks as if he might pass out.

Emmie bolts up from her seat just as Hux shouts, "Don't let the door hit you on the way out, sweetie."

"Oh, I was never your sweetie," Mackenzie fires back. "I was playing you from the beginning. You don't get to tell me to leave. This is *my* town. Every last inch of it belongs to me. You get the hell out, Huxley Baker, and don't you ever let me see your rotten soul again!"

Emmie's hand clutches her throat as she looks to me with sheer panic in her eyes. She knocks over the chair behind her and starts to flail around the room while her eyes enlarge to dangerous heights.

Can't breathe!

"She's choking!" I shout.

And soon, both Leo and Jasper are fighting to wrap their arms around her from behind.

"You're too close to her emotionally," Japer bellows. "I might need to crack a rib," he says as he attempts to give her the Heimlich.

"The hell you're going to crack a rib," Leo roars back as he shoves Jasper off.

All four dogs begin to bark at once as Fish zips over to me.

Don't just stand there, she yowls as Emmie does an odd little dance, her face quickly turning purple. ***Save your best friend, Bizzy! You can't let her die on Christmas Eve!***

Leo and Jasper continue to battle for her, and I waste no time in wrapping my arms around my bestie from behind and giving her three solid squeezes that are, yes, effective enough to crack a soul, let alone a rib. And on the third try, she regurgitates every last bite of that cake in a projectile stream that pins Leo in its wake.

A horrible groan circles the room as Emmie gasps for every breath she can get.

Without hesitating, I yank a bunch of linen napkins off the table and quickly clean the two of them up as Leo quickly sits Emmie back down and gives her some water.

"What the heck happened?" Emmie looks blindsided as her hand continues to pat her throat. "I baked that cake myself. Something must have fallen into the batter."

Leo takes a breath as he holds up a chocolate-covered mess in his hand before quickly rinsing it out in a glass of water on the table.

"This fell into the batter." He sighs as he looks lovingly into Emmie's eyes and drops to one knee.

The room stills around them—with the exception of Hux and Mackenzie who have stooped to slinging expletives at one another, but no one seems to be paying them or their salty language any mind at the moment.

Both Cinnamon and Gatsby come in close and sit by Emmie's feet.

"Elizabeth Lynn Crosby"—tears gloss Leo's eyes as he begins—"I fell in love with you hard and fast. And once that happened, I didn't want to waste a moment. I wanted to make you mine in every single way. You have felt like family to me from the beginning. And today I want to ask you to be my family until the very end—and straight through eternity." He holds up the diamond sparkler. "Will you marry me, Emmie? Will you be my wife?"

Her cheeks pique with color as her lips part. Then, in a moment, she falls on top of him with a hearty embrace.

"Yes!" she beams, and both Cinnamon and Gatsby bark with approval. "I can't believe this." She laughs as he slips the ring onto her finger. "This thing almost killed me."

The room breaks out with cheers and laughter, but the sound of Hux and Mack going at it only seems to escalate.

"Oh hush, all of you," Mackenzie snips, and the room falls quiet once again as she turns her fury back to Hux. "And to think I was actually going to propose to you tonight!"

"What?" he riots the word out. "*You* were going to propose to *me*?" A river of words dam up in his throat. "And to think *I* was going to propose to *you*!"

"What?" she howls right back twice as loud, and perhaps twice as angry. "Don't you dare propose to me, Huxley Baker!"

I catch a glimpse of my sister as she rolls her eyes. ***Get on with it already.***

Hux and Mackenzie stare one another down for a good long while, and the tension between them is palpable.

"*Marry me!*" they both shout at once, and the room holds its collective breath.

"*Fine,*" Mackenzie shouts it out.

"*Fine!*" Hux echoes.

The room breaks out into cheers again, and this time we all take a much-needed deep breath.

Bodies swirl around the room as people congratulate the happy, and the somewhat distressed, couples.

I pull Emmie in for a firm embrace. "It looks as if we've got a wedding to plan."

She sniffs as she wipes the tears from her eyes. "Let's hope the wedding is a lot less dangerous in nature." She looks to Leo. "How about something simple at the inn?"

"It sounds perfect," he tells her.

Jasper and I offer our congratulations to them and attempt to do the same for Hux and Mack, but they're still more or less scowling at one another.

The night wraps up, and Fish, Sherlock Bones, Jasper, and I give Rudolph a heartfelt hug until we meet again, and more than enough kisses to go along with it.

At some point just before midnight, Jasper and I crash on the sofa of our cozy little cottage, each with a cup of eggnog in hand, with me nestled in his arms as we watch the fire die down.

"Merry Christmas," I say as I look up at my gorgeous husband. "Our very first official Christmas together."

"Merry Christmas, beautiful." He lands a kiss to my forehead. "We survived and we thrived." He nods to Fish and Sherlock, asleep under their respective stockings. "We'd better put the treats in those red fuzzy socks before they wake up."

"Hey, that's Santa's job." I give his chest a little scratch. "Speaking of which"—my hand crawls under his shirt—"there's still time to get on that naughty list."

A dark laugh brews in his chest. "I'm all for aiding and abetting." He reaches over and sinks a Santa hat over my head. "I might have a few creative gifts for the naughty girls on my list."

"Oh, really?" My brows hike. "I'm anxious to see what you've got in your bag."

Jasper scoops me up and whisks me over to the tree and nods to the uppermost bough. "Mistletoe."

No sooner do our lips meet up than the sound of bells chiming rings from somewhere up above, and I pull back with wonder.

"I think he's really here," I whisper.

Jasper's lids hood low. "We'd better head to the bedroom and try to work you onto that naughty list before he touches down."

"Let's not rush things. I've already got my big gift anyway." I give the scruff on his cheeks a gentle scratch. "Now let's go put the merry in Christmas."

His lips curve at the thought.

"Merry Christmas, Bizzy." He lands another searing kiss to my lips.

And it is merry, indeed.

We're naughty and nice, and without question, this is the most wonderful time of the year.

Recipe

Country Cottage Café Peppermint Bark

Happy Holidays to all! Bizzy Baker Wilder here! It's December in my world and the Country Cottage Café is serving up every delicious treat you can think of. But one in particular is disappearing quickly—peppermint bark. It is smooth, creamy, chocolatey, and with just the right amount of peppermint. Have I mentioned the crunch factor? This holiday treat really checks off all the boxes. And speaking of boxes, it's the perfect gift to box up and give your friends and neighbors. And best of all, they are easy to make—or at least Emmie tells me. She's the baker, I'm the—well, destroyer of all things edible. But I sure can eat, and this delicious bark is perfect for a holiday party or snacking by the fire. Don't forget to make a little extra. You'll want to have a stash of these around just for yourself. Happy peppermint bark making!

And merry Christmas!

Ingredients

About 30 mini candy canes or 5 standard size
5 cups chocolate chips (Emmie uses semi-sweet)

1 ½ teaspoons peppermint extract (to be divided into ¾ teaspoons twice)

4 cups white chocolate chips

Directions

1. Place candy canes in a plastic bag or between two pieces of parchment paper and crush to pieces with a rolling pin (or whatever destructive method you'd like!)

2. Line a cookie sheet with parchment paper and set aside. (if a cookie sheet does not fit in your freezer, you can use two smaller pans.) *Side note, I told Emmie I thought this was strange since a lot of people have a side-by-side refrigerator but she told me not to worry about it—that you would find something that works.

3. Heat about two inches of water in a saucepan over a low heat until the water is steaming, then place a Pyrex bowl (or any heat-resistant bowl) over the saucepan to create a double boiler. Add half of the semi-sweet chocolate chips to the bowl and stir until melted. Then add the other half slowly, making sure to stir throughout the process until smooth.

4. Stir ¾ teaspoon peppermint extract into the melted semi-sweet chocolate mixture.

5. Once again heat one to two inches of water until steaming and place another heat-resistant bowl over it. Place half of the white chocolate chips in it and stir until melted, then slowly add the rest. Stir until smooth.

6. Pour melted chocolate mixture over the parchment lined cookie sheet. Shake the cookie sheet and tap it over the counter to remove any air bubbles. Use a spatula to spread it evenly across the four corners of the sheet pan. Wait 10 minutes until cool. Freeze for 5 minutes. (All of that freezer trouble for 5 minutes of freezing? Emmie says I'm freaking out over nothing.)

7. Stir in the last ¾ teaspoon of peppermint extract into the melted white chocolate mixture. Spread the melted white chocolate over the semi-sweet layer, spreading evenly with a spatula.

8. It's time for those crushed candy canes! Yay! (Even I can do this part without ruining things. I think.) Sprinkle quickly and evenly over the white chocolate layer, pressing them down gently as you go. You can use parchment to help flatten the candy canes into the white chocolate, or your spatula. You can add as many or as little as you like.

9. Let your bark set up until firm, for one hour at least.

10. Break up your bark into pieces and enjoy!

Happy eating and happy holidays from all of us here at the Country Cottage Inn!

A Note from the Authors

Look for **Sealed with a Hiss (Country Cottage Mysteries 13)** coming up next!

Thank you for reading **A Christmas to Dismember (Country Cottage Mysteries 12).**

Acknowledgements

Thank YOU, the reader, for joining us on this adventure to Cider Cove. We hope you're enjoying the Country Cottage Mysteries as much as we are. Don't miss **<u>Sealed with a Hiss</u>** coming up next. It's Valentine's Day in Cider Cover! Thank you so much from the bottom of our hearts for taking this journey with us. We cannot wait to take you back to Cider Cove!

Special thank you to the following people for taking care of this book—Kaila Eileen Turingan-Ramos, Jodie Tarleton, Margaret Lapointe, Amy Barber, and Lisa Markson. And a very big shout out to Lou Harper of Cover Affairs for designing the world's best covers.

A heartfelt thank you to Paige Maroney Smith for being so amazing in every single way.

And last, but never least, thank you to Him who sits on the throne. Worthy is the Lamb! Glory and honor and power are yours. We owe you everything, Jesus.

About the Author

Bellamy Bloom

Bellamy Bloom is a **USA TODAY** bestselling author who writes cozy mysteries filled with humor, intrigue and a touch of the supernatural. When she's not writing up a murderous storm she's snuggled by the fire with her two precious pooches, chewing down her to-be-read pile and drinking copious amounts of coffee.

Visit her at:

www.authorbellamybloom.com

Addison Moore

Addison Moore is a **New York Times**, **USA TODAY** and **Wall Street Journal** bestselling author who writes mystery, psychological thrillers and romance. Her work has been featured in ***Cosmopolitan*** Magazine. Previously she worked as a therapist on a locked psychiatric unit for nearly a decade. She resides on the West Coast with her husband, four wonderful children, and two dogs where eats too much chocolate and stays up way too late. When she's not writing, she's reading. Addison's Celestra Series has been optioned for film by **20th Century Fox.**

Feel free to visit her at:

www.addisonmoore.com

Made in the USA
Middletown, DE
24 October 2023